Dorothy Andreas.

Dark Enemy

Dark Enemy

By E. J. EDWARDS

1724

LONGMANS, GREEN AND CO.

NEW YORK   LONDON   TORONTO

LONGMANS, GREEN AND CO., INC.
55 FIFTH AVENUE, NEW YORK 3

LONGMANS, GREEN AND CO. LTD.
6 & 7 CLIFFORD STREET, LONDON W 1

LONGMANS, GREEN AND CO.
215 VICTORIA STREET, TORONTO 1

DARK ENEMY

PUBLISHED SIMULTANEOUSLY IN THE DOMINION OF CANADA BY
LONGMANS, GREEN AND CO., TORONTO

FIRST EDITION

LIBRARY OF CONGRESS CATALOG CARD NUMBER 54-10862

Printed in the United States of America

Dark Enemy

Chapter 1

THE woman lay on the operating table, blood welling steadily from between the slack lips.

Dr. Powers straightened up from his examination: the bullet wounds were from a small-calibered gun . . . the woman had a chance. "See if that bullet went through." He pointed at the tightly puckered black spot beneath the right eye. "Cut off her hair." He turned to the other nurse: "Pneumo, Miss Sorrento." She moved quickly at his command, but he kept on talking as though lost in the absorption of his task: "The other bullet—that's the bad one—in the right lung . . . we've got to stop this hemorrhaging. . . ."

Deftly his hands moved, hooking up the needle with the

1

pneumothorax machine, inserting the long needle into the unresisting flesh. . . .

The blood from the unconscious woman's mouth traced an erratic line across her cheek and neck, ending in an ever-widening splotch of red on the white top of the table. . . . "Take care of that bleeding now, Miss Sorrento," he directed.

The nurse swung an instrument into place beside the table and placed a suction tip in the woman's mouth.

Tense silence settled over the room, broken only by the crisp sound of the scissors snipping away the thick black hair in disheveled bunches and tangled strands. . . .

The phone on the night supervisor's desk rang once, shrilly. Sister Martha picked up the receiver.

"Call the technician," came Dr. Powers' crisp order. "A transfusion right away. Set up 1500 c.c.'s to start with."

"Yes, doctor. At once." She swung about in her chair: "The lab," she called out to the switchboard operator.

Swiftly the connection was made and the information relayed.

She put down the receiver, but her hand stayed at the side of it, waiting, ready. The lobby was deserted, and it made her strangely uneasy to see its familiar, well-lighted expanse so silent and empty. Her thought went to the room, back there in the depth of the building, where a doctor and two nurses had come to grips with death. . . . The officers, who had brought in the patient, had assured her that they knew the woman and that she had no religion—no nothing. . . . "Just a tramp," one of them blurted out, and then turned a furious red, remembering to whom he was speaking. . . .

"Will you want Father Chriswell, Sister?" called out the switchboard operator.

Sister Martha's eyes darted to the desk clock. . . . 2:15 A.M. . . . It was very late and the chaplain was no longer a young man. She turned slightly, speaking over her shoulder: "Not yet. If she takes a turn for the worse— Dr. Powers will let us know. . . ."

Sister Liboria pushed open the swinging doors and wheeled her medical cart into the shadowy silence of the emergency room. Overhead lamps made a little island of radiance in the center of the room. A limp body lay on the table, a thing of bloodied flesh, disheveled hair and shuddering breath. . . .

The Sister's eyes went inquiringly to Dr. Powers, and he nodded assent for her to start the transfusion: "She is still in shock. We'll want an I.V., too, Sister." He spoke clearly, and the steadiness of his voice seemed to dispel the shadowy fear and evil that hung over the room.

As the Sister moved swiftly to her task, she noticed the reek of liquor from the woman's open mouth. It was like a stain in the clean antiseptic odors of the room. Low, confused, animal-like sounds kept coming from the woman's throat, and her lips incessantly lifted, baring her teeth. Suddenly the sounds became words, grating, savage words—a curse—and then a tortured cry: "It hurts, hurts! . . . Stop . . . stop it, stop it!"

She put a quieting hand on the woman's cheek: "You must try to be quiet," she admonished gently, ". . . we are trying to help—"

The woman's head lunged upwards. With a convulsive snap, her strong white teeth bit deep into the Sister's forearm.

At her startled cry, the nurses dropped their tasks, and came to her help. They pried at the woman's clenched teeth and the locked jaws; but like a scavenging dog worrying a bone, she held on, moaning, snarling, tenacious.

Dr. Powers' voice cut sharply through the confusion: "Here, nurse—hold this." Miss Sorrento jumped to his side and grasped the needle from his hand. He pushed the other nurse aside, but before he could do anything further, a strange, strangled sort of cry erupted from the woman, her teeth released their hold, and a gush of blood belched from her mouth. With the abruptness of a snapped bowstring, her whole body went slack, the tongue rolled out of her bloodied mouth, and the shorn head slid to one side. . . .

The Sister swayed slightly backwards, and Dr. Powers' hand reached out quickly, steadying her.

She stood there a moment, staring unbelievingly at her mangled arm, then she drew a shaky breath and looked up at him: "I'm . . . I'm all right," she assured him.

He spun about and rapped out an order. Miss Smith ran to one of the cabinets. He took the syringe from her and swiftly injected the heart stimulant. He straightened up, lifted the woman's hand, and felt for the pulse.

They stood there—the doctor, the nurses, the Sister—in-

4

tently watching the woman's face. And as they watched, a change took place. Slowly, as though some invisible chemistry were at work, a smoothness came over the contorted countenance, wiping away its fury of fear and struggle and pain. The blood-drained flesh of the face settled into a mask of dead grayness—and everything was ended. The woman was one with the desert dust. . . .

Dr. Powers handed the empty syringe to the nurse at his side, and turned to the Sister: "That arm of yours, Sister . . ." he suggested and nodded towards a small service table.

She removed the bloodied muslin sleevelet, and he peered at the lacerated flesh. His lips tightened, and the Sister caught the half-smothered expression of anger.

"She didn't know what she was doing," she said defensively.

He looked up at her: at her eyes soft with compassion. "No, of course not," he agreed quickly. "She didn't."

He picked up a bottle and immersed a swab in it, "This is going to hurt a bit, Sister," he cautioned and began to disinfect the wound. She did not flinch. He tossed the swab aside. His eyes lifted to her face: her eyes were closed, her cheeks very white. "Do you feel faint, Sister?" he asked with sudden concern. Her eyes flew open and she stared at him uncomprehendingly. "I asked if you were faint," he repeated.

"Oh, no, doctor." Color suddenly flooded her cheeks. "I'm perfectly all right."

His intent gaze seemed to deepen her embarrassment. Slowly his eyes came away. He picked up a roll of gauze and

5

began to bandage the wound. His head was slightly inclined: "Sorry, Sister," he apologized in a low voice. "I did not realize what you were doing—she could use a prayer, I guess."

"I wasn't praying; that is—not exactly, doctor."

Again he looked up at her and, for a moment, he seemed about to ask her something. Instead he turned away: "I'll want to change that dressing tomorrow, Sister. Drop in to see me before you go on duty in the morning." He turned to one of the nurses and directed her to help the Sister with her medical cart.

He watched them go from the room, then picked up the phone and called the desk: "Sister Martha? That gunshot case: we've lost her. . . . I'm sorry; I couldn't notify you sooner. It went very fast. Hemorrhage. I'll be along in a few minutes and fill out the report."

He replaced the receiver, went to a basin and began to scrub his hands energetically. The sound of the splashing water seemed incongruously loud. He looked over his shoulder. The other nurse was there: Miss Sorrento. She was standing in front of one of the cabinets, her back to him, and she was perfectly still—strangely still.

He snatched up a towel and went towards her. "Rather a messy case, Sandra," he observed, making a show of toweling his hands. "She had only a slim chance, and she—"

"You didn't have to let her die like a dog!"

His hands were suddenly tight knots, hidden in the crumpled towel. For a long moment he stared at her rigid

6

back: "I thought," he said with slow emphasis, "that we had settled that matter . . . months ago."

She turned slowly to face him: "Months ago . . .?" There was a look of dull wonderment in her face. "This—?" One hand fluttered in a gesture towards the table and its burden of death.

His eyes held hers in a long glance. "You haven't forgotten, have you?"

The way he stressed the words brought it back to her in a rush; and shame reddened the smooth white cheeks. Abruptly her gaze dropped away, but not before he had seen the stricken look that filled her eyes.

The towel slipped unheeded from his hands as he reached forward and took gentle hold of her shoulders. She stood unresponsive, her head bowed:

"I . . . I forgot myself again," she admitted dully. "I'm sorry." Her voice had the toneless quality of a child reciting a hated lesson: "I'm sorry," she repeated; and then abruptly her eyes darted up to his: "I can keep on saying that all night long, but it will not do any good, will it?" She twisted away from under his hands, turning her back to him: "It's no use," she said despairingly, "I can never get away from what I am . . . never."

"You are what you will to be."

She shook her head in angry denial: "I wanted to be different, but I'm not. I'm the same. Nothing's changed. I was a fool to think I could change. I'll never change. I'll always be the same. There's no hope for people like me. . . ."

He waited, giving her mood of bitter self-pity a chance to evaporate. Then he spoke: "I think there's all the hope in the world for you." The quiet assurance of his words caused her to turn slowly. He saw the doubt in her eyes, the questioning: "Yes, I mean that," he assured her. "You know I do. . . . These past weeks you have come a long way, Sandra—"

"I have been trying, doctor," she cut in quickly, "really I have. I . . . I was sort of proud of myself—but this—this happened so quickly—" She could not go on. Excuses were no good. They never were. When a thing was done, it was done.

"I know, Sandra," he nodded, "and I understand. But others might not. So you must be on your guard always. You can never allow yourself to blurt out opinions of that sort before others. It would ruin you. You must remember that."

For a moment the warm choking feeling in her throat made it impossible to answer. She wanted to tell him so much, and she could not. Not now; perhaps never. . . . "Yes," she finally managed, "I'll remember . . . always."

He was pleased, and, for some unaccountable reason, grateful. "Get to work now," he admonished, and his encouraging smile told her that the incident was closed. . . .

Obediently, Sandra set about picking up instruments and placing them in the sterilizer, her mood of rebellion gone, eclipsed by the memory of his smile. She had never ceased wondering how even a faint smile changed his appearance so completely. It seemed to kindle a spark of boyishness in his wide-set blue eyes and made one forget, for the moment, the

8

severe, sharp lines of the jaw and cleft chin. . . . Automatically, her hands kept gathering up the soiled instruments and putting things back in their assigned places, but her heart moved in a little world apart, in the light and warmth of the time when first he had smiled on her. . . .

She had been a terrified girl then. To have everyone condemning you, unjustly, with silent looks and studied aloofness, is a crushing experience. For her, who had labored, so hard and long, to gain a position of respectability, it was doubly devastating. It seemed only adding cruelty to injustice to subject her to this before expelling her. . . .

When finally Dr. Powers summoned her to his office, what was she expected to think? He was a member of the staff; he had been an eye-witness of her blunder—she could only surmise that he had been delegated to pronounce upon her the hospital's verdict of expulsion.

Keyed up to a high pitch of defiance, she had faced him, ready for anything and everything—except what he had actually said: "I pleaded with the staff, and they have agreed, conditionally, to grant you another chance. . . ."

Perhaps the period of fear and waiting, the strain of being an object of silent disgrace had slightly unhinged her. There was no other way to explain the words which had spilled from her lips, the cynical observation about men who did favors: "There is always a price tag attached—and what was his?"

How unlovely she must have seemed to him at that moment! And yet, how generous and patient he had been. Knowing all, he could forgive all—and, in her blindness, that had been the final effrontery! What did he *know* about her? How could he dare to make such an arrogant statement? Had he ever tried to make a dying mother's last moments easy—and then been punished for it! Had he been treated like an outcast because he had been honest?

Her impassioned words left him unmoved. They were like arrows splintering against a rock. He told her what he knew about her—and he knew everything: her efforts to support and care for a sick and widowed mother by taking a job as a night-club entertainer; the degrading, sly innuendoes of the patrons, their leering eyes, the ever-recurring invitations . . . her own loathing of it all—

The detailed knowledge he had of her emotions, her fears and hopes, struck her dumb. Fearfully, she had looked at him, wondering how he had unearthed all her close-held secrets. Now, of course, she felt certain that in his concern for her he must have gone to the Superioress of the Hospital. She knew: her mother, while a patient here, had told her all; and the good nun had allayed her mother's sharpest anxiety by offering Sandra a chance to enter their school for nurses. How determinedly she had tried to measure up to the opportunity! And she had. They had been pleased with her work; she had justified all their hopes—up to that terrible moment when her mother lay twisting about in her final agony. . . .

Dr. Powers had been present then. He knew what had happened. He had seen how she screamed at the doctor in charge, begging, demanding that he end her mother's suffering: accusing him of treating animals more mercifully than human beings. . . .

It had not been just hysteria. Foolishly, she had made it plain that it was, too, conviction. Everyone knew that, and because of it condemned her. He alone had not looked on her as some inhuman monster. Of all those good people, he alone seemed able to repudiate her convictions, and yet be concerned about her as a person. . . .

With painstaking care Sandra finished putting the room to rights. She found a pleasure now in the routine little task: she was doing what he wanted her to do. His slightest wish had the strange power of investing even her simplest task with importance. In the past weeks, the thought of him had, time and again, invaded her mind while at work. With no deliberate intent it had grown into a habit. And now it was like a quiet little place inside of her to which she could withdraw at will and be content. . . .

How often she returned in memory to the things he had told her and tried to explain to her: *Suffering was not the sort of evil she thought it to be; it held deep and mysterious possibilities.* . . . The words meant little to her and all his attempts at explanation made only one thing clear: these were beliefs he prized deeply—and he wanted to share them with her!

In the poverty-stricken days of childhood, how many times she had stood outside a store window, her face pressed to the glass, dazzled by the splendor outspread before her. Desire was like a hot greedy flame in her heart, feeding on things beyond her reach, eternally beyond her reach—until the moment she had met him. . . .

11

What Dr. Powers had reported to the staff about her, she did not know, but she had been allowed to finish her training and graduate.

She paused before one of the cabinets. Her image looked back at her from the glassed-in front: the dark hair and eyes, the lips finely touched with crimson. . . . It was an attractive face, she knew, if she did not allow temper and sullenness to mar it. Why had she allowed that momentary mood of rebellion to lay hold of her? Would she never learn to control herself? to be like him? This was all she asked of life: to be like him; to walk at his side; along the same path as he, sharing fully his serenity and strength, one with him, in everything. . . .

The instruments clattered noisily from her hands on to the glass shelf of the cabinet. Reality was something she could never escape; and the reality stood mercilessly clear before her. He had not the faintest idea of what he had come to mean to her, nor how she now felt about him. He did not know she existed—not in that way. He was married.

She closed the instrument cabinet with sudden and unnecessary force. It made a sharp angry sound in the silent room. She spun about, and stood there, aware again of the cold, almost evil emptiness of the place.

Slowly she went over to the table, and looked down at the dead woman: a small cold silence on a small cold table. The woman must have been young and pretty once, and this was how it had all ended: sightless eyes, unfeeling flesh.

Bitterness and revolt came surging back into her heart.

Life was all a little game, soon ended, and you were a fool not to get from it the most you could, no matter who got hurt or how. The one and only thing that made sense was to see that your own needs and desires were fulfilled. . . .

The door of the room suddenly swung open and Father Chriswell hurried in. His white hair was disheveled from sleep, but there was a wide-awake urgency in the straight-shouldered way he crossed the room. He stopped at the table and looked down on the woman. After a moment, his head lifted and he turned his deeply shadowed eyes on Sandra: "I got here as quickly as I could—" There was distress in his voice.

"She was out of her head—violent," Sandra offered. "There wasn't anything you could have done."

He made no reply. He had turned back to the table, and his hands were busy doing ritualistic little things, swiftly and yet reverently. After a while he stopped, closed his eyes, and bowed his head.

Sandra watched him. He was praying. What use would that be now? The woman had died like an animal, snarling and bloodied, fighting the very ones who had tried to help her. Prayer could not change that fact. Yet there the chaplain stood praying, as though the story was not yet ended, as though there was something beyond sight and sound, beyond flesh and blood and death. . . . It was the same kind of faith that breathed in Dr. Powers' behavior, although he was not a Catholic. It was the same kind of world in which he lived. And when he was near it seemed real, but when he was not,

it all crumbled away. It seemed only words again, now that
he was gone. But, she told herself, it was right, it had to be
right. If Dr. Powers found in it the source for his strength
and goodness, it had to be right—and she would thrust her
way into it, possess it, no matter what the cost. . . .

Chapter 2

THE morning paper had the story. Father Chriswell read it slowly, sadly. All the pitiful facts of the woman's life were there . . . and they all added up to a single conclusion: she had died as she had lived . . . sordidly.

He pushed the paper aside. The account distressed him, because he saw beyond the lurid details to the real tragedy: to the moments of grace, the flashes of warning that had surely come, time and again, and that had been, time and again, rejected. And he could not quite wholly subdue the feeling of disappointment for having arrived too late to help her. Not that he had any illusions about his own abilities. He had no particular gift of persuasiveness. But at the final moment, when pain had crumbled her pride, she might have listened. For pain had an eloquence all its own: it was a harsh teacher, but its rough hand had a mysteriously softening touch. He knew . . . how well he knew!

His eyes lifted to the books that filled the shelves on the far side of the room. They were freshly jacketed books, new books, all bearing the same design and title—his book. Years of work—and one single book! "Logically coherent . . . brilliantly conclusive . . . scholastically sound . . . penetrating. . . ." The theological reviews had not been sparing of praise. But they had not told all—it had no readers.

Naïvely, he had imagined that here in the hospital there would be eager interest in the things he had written. His lips twisted wryly. People came to a hospital, he had learned, to get rid of their suffering, not to read books about the metaphysics of it. One doctor had borrowed a copy and read it, but his interest had been purely academic. . . .

Through the open window came the wail of the ambulance's siren, filling the room with its ominous urgency. He pushed back from the desk and crossed the room. The morning was a miracle of soft golden haze. How freshly soft and beautiful the days opened up in this desert world, giving no hint of the heat-deadened hours that were to follow. . . . In the far distance the gray ghostly tips of the city's buildings thrust upwards through the haze: turrets of sorrow piercing life's wonder and joy. . . .

Again there came the cry of the siren, rising with slowly increasing stridency, like some tormented soul being swept up a flaming ascent of suffering. Abruptly, it fell away, in a long, drawn-out, dying moan. . . .

Into the eyes of the priest came a strangely tortured look. . . . All his priestly life he had wanted to be an apostle, and instead he had been a teacher. ". . . There are different kinds of service . . . and there are different manifestations of power, though it is the same God who manifests his power everywhere in all of us." The words of the great Apostle had helped subdue the insistent desire for apostolic actualities, but this recent assignment as hospital chaplain had caused the banked up fires to break forth into open conflagration. . . . The work he had always craved, he now had—and he could not handle it.

Somehow he had to reach all these needy ones: he had to learn the broad human approach; somehow he had to give them the truths he had discovered. But how? . . . How talk about causes when people were only concerned with effects? How did you go about giving what no one wanted? . . .

The voice of the siren was still. The ambulance had arrived. Another pain-torn body was being carried through the doors that were never locked. Again the hospital's ponderous machinery of healing was being set in motion. . . .

From a drawer he took a small stole, folded it and put it in the pocket of his cassock. On top of the desk was a slip of paper holding a list of names, and in back of each name was a room number.

A name and a number. That was all it was, a list of names and numbers, but he knew that as he knocked at each door and was admitted to a room, the name soon became a reality, confronting him again with the age-old mystery of suffering. Drunkards, narcotic addicts, attempted suicides, victims of

17

fights and accidents and fires . . . they were all here. His little list of names and numbers was a horrible concentration of life's conflicting madness. . . .

From room to room he went, moving in a little world of his own, yet a world that was related to the hospital's swirling activity. Doctors, nurses, orderlies, technicians greeted him, turned to watch him as he halted before the door of a room. They observed the momentary pause, the fleeting expression that twisted his lips and tightened his lean jaws . . . then the resolute lifting of the square shoulders before entering the room. And some of them wondered idly whether his unremitting care of the sick had built up in him some interior repugnance for the work. . . . But his eyes never gave any indication of inner conflict. Face to face with a patient he spoke softly and listened patiently, he chided gently and encouraged, he donned his stole and forgave, he kept it in his pocket and sadly prayed.

When he came to the last name on his list he was utterly tired. He had done a full morning's work. This final patient . . . Mrs. Joyce Blake . . . he felt tempted to postpone till later in the day.

A nurse went by trundling a cart fitted with racks displaying magazines and books. For a moment his gaze followed it broodingly, then he spun about and started for Mrs. Blake's room. . . .

The landing at the top of a flight of steps had been walled off with screens. Through a small opening between the end screen and the wall, Father Chriswell entered the little enclosure. In a corner was a bed and a chair. A large window opened up on an outside balcony. There was no ornamentation except a little spray of flowers on the side table.

He walked up to the side of the bed. She was a fragile-looking little person: the schoolgirl braids with their bits of bright yellow ribbon, the frank interested gaze of the wide blue eyes—she seemed but a child.

He returned her greeting and took a chair at the side of the bed. . . . It was difficult to believe that such a slight creature had been through so much: tuberculosis; the long months of the cure; her present pregnancy, and with it a recurrence of her illness. . . . And yet the untroubled eyes gave no hint of the hourly agony of apprehension, of waiting and fearing, which he knew must be her lot.

He drew the tasselled edge of his cincture across his lap: "The head nurse tells me you had a bad night, Mrs. Blake," he began.

She nodded assent. "My breathing, Father," she explained. "I had some trouble with it. But it's all right now. They gave me oxygen."

It was evident that all was not right. Her breathing was still labored. He waited for her to unburden herself of the dread, the destroying fear. . . .

She smiled at him: "Would you mind calling me Joyce? Everyone else does . . . it seems I'm going to be here a long time."

"Thank you, Joyce; I'll do that." In her simplicity she seemed not to know what trials still lay ahead. He had to prepare her to meet them: "Your sickness is a cross, Joyce," he began gravely, "and at times it may get so heavy that you don't know what to do with it. . . . You can't really do anything with it—no one can—unless you learn to carry it with the One who carried the cross of all our sorrow and suffering. . . ."

The trusting expectancy in her eyes halted him. How could he in a few sentences convey to her the truths that had taken him years to learn? . . . His lips moved, soundlessly, in a desperate prayer for help . . . and then, hesitantly, he began to explain: how little it would take to change everything; a brief act of the will, a submission, a joining of her will to His, a desire to be one with Him in this aspect of her life as in all aspects of her life. . . . The mystery of love was here: the mystery of oneness, and the mystery of greatness; the suffering becoming a sacrament, as it were, a means for a divine quality to flow into her . . . the strength of the Loved flowing into the lover . . . and the lover beginning to act as the Loved, with His patience, and generosity, and yes—divineness, "because it is not just you, but the Loved one, living in you, who does these things. . . ."

He paused, realizing he had said a great deal, and he had said nothing: "You can't grasp all this now," he admitted slowly, "but if you will—"

"Oh, but I do, Father," she broke in quickly, "I do." He looked up at her, startled. "Truly I do, Father," she persisted. "I read all about it in your book."

She turned and picked up a book from her bedside table.

"See? I have been reading it again. It helped me so much that I felt sure it would help him, too."

With incredulous eyes he looked from the book to her: "Him?" he asked blankly.

"Dr. Powers," she explained. "Last night, when I had trouble breathing, he stayed with me, for a long time, even after it was not necessary. . . . I thought it was to reassure me. But it wasn't. He was puzzled . . . about me."

"You mean your condition had him worried?" asked the priest hesitantly.

"Oh, no, not that. It was because I did not want to take the oxygen. He was angry because I wouldn't take it. And I was so short of breath that I could not get out the words to explain why I did not want it. But he finally understood. I was afraid the oxygen might endanger the child." She smiled up at him. "I'm terribly ignorant about such things."

He looked at her wonderingly. The maternal instinct was a selfless one, and yet, more than once, he had seen how panic-stricken a patient became when breathing difficulties arose. . . . "Under the circumstances, Joyce, you can't blame Dr. Powers for being puzzled."

She grasped his meaning, but shook her head in denial: "It wasn't that, Father. It was the beads—the rosary beads. . . . I was holding them in my hand all the time—and I showed them to him when he asked me if I was afraid. . . ."

Father Chriswell's eyebrows lifted: "Surely he knew what the beads were for."

"Oh, yes. He knew that. But he could not see how they could keep me from being afraid. . . . He wanted to know if praying did anything to the pain."

He murmured something about "the scientific mind being an inquiring one," but it was only to cover the slight shock of surprise that her words had sent through him. After reading his book, Dr. Powers had asked that same question of him . . . and he had seemed satisfied with the explanation given then. . . . "Did you enlighten his ignorance?" he asked.

"I told him some of the things I remembered from your book."

"What did he say?"

"Nothing. But he smiled, sort of gratefully. Do you think I should give him the book to read, Father?"

The priest shook his head: "He has read the book."

Her eyes widened in disbelief: "But he couldn't have," she objected, ". . . he couldn't have. . . ." And when Father Chriswell assured her again that he had read the book, from cover to cover, an almost pathetic blankness came over her countenance. It lasted only a moment. With swift intuition she grasped the reason for Dr. Powers' innocent little stratagem: he was just being his usual considerate self. Another person would have quickly put her in her place—but not he. He was a treasure. . . . Her voice took on a warm enthusiasm as she recounted how patient he had been with her. She had been so disturbed about the child—whether she would be able to have it or not, whether it would be healthy—and

22

he had quieted all her fears. Her confidence in him was complete. . . . She paused a moment: "But wait till I see him!" she threatened smilingly. "Letting me prattle away, while he sat there like a little boy listening to his teacher—you would really have thought it was something entirely new I was telling him."

"Maybe it was."

The dry little comment wiped all the animation from Joyce's face.

"You might have said it in a different way," he hastened to explain, "a way he could understand."

"But I understood what you wrote, Father," she protested quickly, "and surely he would. Sister says he has a brilliant mind."

"Yes," he readily admitted, "he has. The Chief-of-Staff, Dr. Bromwell, considers him the brightest doctor the hospital has. His medical training and knowledge are of the very best."

He had spoken without any particular emphasis but she grasped the implication in back of his words: Complete though Dr. Powers' medical knowledge was, he was only now beginning to sense and seek even more vital realities. Knowing so much, he yet knew so little. . . . "Father, I'd give anything to help him!"

He smiled at her vehemence: "I thought I was here to discuss you—not Dr. Powers."

A tinge of color came into her cheeks: "But I have no problems, Father," she objected, "and *he* has—" A look of wonder-

23

ment came over the priest's face: she was so evidently sincere in what she had said. "Can't you help him, Father?" she pleaded.

"You can't force these things, Joyce," he said quietly. "After reading the book, Dr. Powers asked a great many questions. I answered as best I could. He seemed satisfied."

Joyce's eyes clouded over with thought: "Why does he come to me then, and ask the same questions?" Her gaze lifted: "Why did he do that, Father?"

He turned away from the honest wonderment showing in her face and picked up the book from the table. "Perhaps," he said slowly, "your explanation had something mine did not have."

His fingers riffled the pages. There were no pencil marks on the margins, but the book had been well-thumbed. . . . Written words were dead things; the one and only dynamic teacher was living behavior. . . .

"You're not well, are you, Father?" The irrelevant remark brought his head sharply upright. Openly concerned, her childlike eyes were studying him: "Shouldn't you see a doctor?" she ventured hesitantly.

The humor of it struck him: he, the consoler, was being consoled! "I'm afraid," he said gravely, "no doctor has a cure for my ailment." The sudden apprehension in her face brought a twinkle into his eyes: "A man should learn what people read," he explained, "before he writes a book."

"But, Father, I love your book," she protested, swiftly and sincerely. "It has done so much for me. My life used to be all daydreams: about some party I was going to; some dress I

had to get . . . things like that. That's all changed now."
She hesitated. "Well, not entirely—but at least those things
are not important any more. Only the present seems to
count . . . and there's a sort of deeper feel to everything. . . ." She looked up at him and her lips were parted in
a little smile: "Isn't it strange that I had to get sick in order
to learn how to live? But you found that out before I did. In
the book, you said: 'You can see farther through a tear than
a telescope.' It's the truth, Father."

He stood up slowly. "Thank you, Joyce," he said humbly,
"for proving it to me."

Chapter 3

THE light from the reading lamp threw a pool of radiance
over the desk's polished surface. There was a slip of
paper lying there, and it seemed suddenly to have caught
Dr. Powers' attention. He picked it up, and, for a moment,
was obviously absorbed in what the bit of paper held.

Dr. Ralph Reynolds stopped speaking. He had said enough
anyhow—perhaps, too much. Nervously, he scrubbed his
stubby fingers through his closely cut hair. Being still young,
he had his own little private pantheon of heroes: and in it
Gray Powers held an exalted place. Gray knew his medicine,
and he knew people; he was sure of himself; he abided by the
rules and yet he was liberal—that is, in some respects he was

liberal. On some things he was like a rock. For that reason you had to speak carefully if you discussed a difficulty with him. Ralph felt he had been careful: he had proposed his problem without giving the least inkling of his own personal feelings—at least he did not think he had. . . .

Gray's silence bothered him: he wondered what it was on that bit of paper that could have brought such a look of satisfaction into his friend's usually impassive countenance. . . . He cleared his throat: "What's your opinion of the whole thing, Gray?"

He had blurted out the question more loudly than he had intended, but it brought Gray out of his abstracted mood: "There's nothing much to be said, Ralph," he replied quietly, "except"—his fingers were mechanically folding the paper into small exact squares—"your diagnosis could be wrong."

Ralph shook his head: "It was right. I checked with Dr. Bromwell."

"Well? What are you worrying about then?"

Indignation filled Ralph's voice. "Weren't you listening to what I told you?"

"Why, yes . . . I was listening."

"Didn't you understand: it's either the mother or the child!"

"Yes, I understood that clearly enough," replied Gray evenly. . . . He looked at the younger doctor intently a moment, then turned and dropped the folded slip of paper on the desk. He spoke over his shoulder: "Medical ethics treats this problem of yours, you know, exactly and in detail."

"I've read the books," replied Ralph with a trace of impatience, "but what good are books when you're up against the real thing? This is different."

Dr. Powers was silent for a while. "Yes," he finally agreed, "it is. It always is, when you meet up with the real thing." He seemed to be weighing the matter in his own mind, and, after a while, he turned and faced the young doctor: "Just what is it that you want me to do?" he finally asked. "It's your case, you know. *You* will have to make the ultimate decision."

"I know that," answered Ralph in a harassed voice. "I've made the decision—or perhaps I should say I had the decision made for me. The woman wants to have the child."

"That's her right and privilege," replied Dr. Powers swiftly.

"Of course," agreed Ralph, "I know that."

"Why all the worry then?" He flung out his hands. "She's made her decision: that ends the matter for you."

"It should, but it doesn't," came the stubborn denial, and for a moment Ralph studied, with unseeing eyes, his stubby, capable fingers. Abruptly he jerked them upwards and scrubbed them nervously through his hair. Finally he lifted his gaze. "Look, Gray, I know there are quite a few doctors in this hospital who are supposed to be model Christians, but there isn't one of them to whom I'd tell the funny ideas I've gotten about this case."

"But you are going to confide them to me, because"—Gray's eyebrows lifted slightly—"I'm not a 'model Christian'?"

"Maybe," agreed Ralph with slow emphasis, "and then

28

again maybe it's because I think you're the right kind of Christian."

Gray's firm lips relaxed in a slight smile: "It sounds like some sort of compliment, but I think the logic is a bit involved."

"I can put it plainer. You've got the right kind of slant on things."

"Things? What things?"

"Ethics, religion, well—life."

"I thought I was a doctor."

"That was understood. I meant that in the first place. That's why I'm asking your help." He stopped, and nervously cleared his throat: "There are times when I don't know if I'm on foot or on horseback in this hospital. You see, I did everything right in this case—I mean right according to the hospital's ideas. But what I got to thinking was this: would I have acted the same way if it was my own wife who was the patient?"

Gray's bland "I didn't know you were married" brought a quick spark of irritation into Ralph's eyes.

"I'm not, and you know I'm not. But if I were, I wouldn't let my wife make that kind of decision. I'd save her life . . . no matter what the books say."

"And kill your own child?"

For a moment the gaze of the two men were locked fast; then Ralph's eyes dropped away from the accusing glance of his friend.

After a moment of stiff silence, Gray walked over to the

desk, spun the chair around and sat down in it facing the crestfallen young culprit: "Look, Ralph," he began, "you must never let emotion sway you in a case of this kind. You've got to go by facts, and the facts of the matter are that the unborn child is a human being with a right to life. Because its presence endangers the life of the mother, do you think that gives you the right to kill it? Any direct attack upon a child's life is criminal. It makes you a murderer, just as sure as if that child were up and walking about."

"I know, I know," replied Dr. Reynolds almost sullenly, "it says all that in the ethics book. But this is only a human being in embryo—the child hasn't been born yet."

"Birth doesn't make it a human being," came the quick reply, "conception does." He hesitated a moment. "At least that is the opinion on which this hospital bases its procedure."

For a long while Ralph was silent. When he spoke some of the assurance had gone out of his voice: "Maybe you're right, Gray, but—well—I don't know." His head came up and his clear young gaze was directed fully at Dr. Powers. "Tell me, Gray, just between ourselves, would you follow out that line if it were a question of your own wife?"

"Of course. So would you."

The young man stared at him a moment, as though not completely sure that Dr. Powers was serious. Then he shook his head. "You're over-rating me, Gray. Thanks; but I'm not that kind of a man."

"What kind are you?"

"Just a doctor, not a hero."

"Sometimes it's the same thing." He walked away. "When you took the Hippocratic oath—"

The sound of a knock interrupted what he was about to say. He crossed quickly to the door and opened it. Sandra stood there holding a tray. He held the door wide, and she murmured a formal little greeting as she entered. Ralph's eyes flicked up to her a moment and then back to Dr. Powers. He stood up.

Dr. Powers put a friendly hand on his shoulder as they walked towards the door. "We can discuss the matter some more later on, if you wish." Outside the door he detained him a moment: "The basis of any decisions you have to make, Ralph, as you will eventually discover, is you yourself, and you are made up of the things you believe in deeply, the principles you live by."

"I'm beginning to understand that, Gray," he replied seriously. "But how do you tell the true from the false, the feelings from the facts?"

Gray smiled indulgently: "Time will take care of that for you," he assured him.

His step, as he came back into the room, was unhurried. Sandra liked the way he moved, easily and with a certain deliberateness. Although he was tall and broad-shouldered and solidly fleshed, yet there was no awkwardness about him. His gestures were few and his voice quiet. It was a deceptive stolidity, hiding, as she knew, a great warmth of understanding and kindliness.

He spread his napkin and began to pour a cup of coffee. . . . "How does it happen that you are on the tray detail this evening, Sandra?"

"The student nurse is ill, doctor," she replied. "I'm assigned to general duty tonight, but since I don't go on for another half hour, Sister asked me to bring you your tray." He was busily engaged in eating, unaware of how eager she was to have him talk to her. "Doctor—" He looked up at the sudden intensity in her voice. "I'm sorry about what happened the other night in the emergency room, really I am."

Her attempt to engage his interest failed. "That's over and done with, Sandra," he said, and turned back to his meal.

"I know, but not what caused it. It almost seems that the things I went through before I came here will never stop influencing me: the people I associated with, the things they said and believed—it's like a wound. It's closed over, but it's always there. And it's ugly."

"It's a healthy scar, Sandra. Don't open it. Leave it alone. Forget it."

"I want to," she replied fervently. "I really want to."

He caught the quick movement of her hand as it lifted to touch the gold and white pin affixed to her uniform, and the significance of the little action suddenly held him. . . . She had seemed such a lonely, lost little thing on the day she received that coveted nurse's pin; surrounded by joyful classmates she alone had no one with whom to share her Commencement Day joy. . . . Acting *in loco parentis* had been a new experience for him. At the time he had felt rather self-conscious, and as a result he could think of nothing to

say except some stereotyped things about her newly con-
ferred nurse's pin being not just an emblem of respectability,
but a badge of selfless devotion to the sick and suffering. . . . Surprisingly, she had not only remembered his
words, but was trying to live up to them. . . . "It takes a
lot of courage, Sandra," he observed, "to follow out an idea
to its conclusion."

Swift pleasure lit up her countenance. "But that is the difference between mediocrity and greatness. The truly great
person is one who has laid hold of a great idea and never lets
go until the idea has become a reality."

Speechless, he stared at her. As far as he could recall he
had voiced that opinion only once in her presence; and to
find her reciting it to him now, almost word for word, was
more than startling. To cover up his vague unease he made
a show of addressing his attention to his meal. . . . The
muted sound of a bell filtered into the room's silence. Sandra
put down the napkin she had been folding. "That's the chapel
bell, doctor. May I go?"

He looked up: "Chapel? . . . I thought you were going
on duty soon."

She smiled. "This won't take but ten minutes. It's Bene-
diction. I . . . I started going several days ago . . . after
that promise I made you in the emergency room. It helps
me to remember."

He nodded gravely: "Surely, Sandra. Run along. You can
pick up the tray when you return."

With a smile of gratitude she turned and left the room.

For some time Dr. Powers sat there staring at the door

through which she had taken her leave. The meal seemed to be forgotten. He tossed his napkin on the tray, rose and went over to his desk.

The slip of paper, which he had folded during his talk with Ralph, lay there. He picked it up and unfolded it. It was a memorandum from the office: Dr. Bromwell wanted to see him before he went on duty. . . . As a rule, the Chief-of-Staff used the phone for discussing routine matters. . . . This summons to a personal conference had the earmarks of something truly important.

He coiled his stethoscope, thrust it into the pocket of his jacket, and went from the room.

Chapter 4

IT stood on the edge of the town, where the streets ended and the desert began: a fit place for a hospital. The sun was below the western horizon, and the long white building stood stockinged in shadow—a somber thing of mystery, half shadow, half light. . . .

Gray's hands rested lightly on the wheel, guiding the car with small, automatic touches. Some pleasurable thought seemed to have cast over him a mood of deep contentment. His eyes held a faraway look, and a faint smile of satisfaction hovered about his lips.

But the thin-faced man at his side was no respecter of moods: "Neither fish nor flesh," growled Dr. Hilary Arnet disgustedly. "It's not fully a church, nor exclusively a hospital."

Gray did not reply, but his attention focused on the building that reared its walls so sturdily in the day's dying light. Again Arnet spoke, drawing out his words pensively, sarcastically:

"'As simple as a dove, and as wise as a serpent. . . .'"

Faint amusement showed in Gray's face: "Since when did you start quoting Scripture?"

Arnet's thin blue eyes flashed a look at him: "You don't have a monopoly on that."

Laughingly, Gray admitted that he did not. "But I never thought my conduct would affect you. . . . Have I made a convert?"

He knew what the answer to his question would be, but Arnet's grunt of disdain was much more forceful than he had expected. He sighed defeatedly:

"You are a very unrealistic realist, Hil," he complained.

"That," stated Arnet dogmatically, "is where you are wrong. My opposition to what you are trying to do has a very realistic basis: *it will not work.*" He drew out a cigar and held it by the tip, waggling it up and down as though it were a pointer. "The direct approach . . . always," he counseled. ". . . Go straight forward . . . head-on. . . . That's the way to get—"

"A brain concussion," broke in Gray dryly.

Arnet's cold blue eyes flashed a rapier glance at him. Gray had seen that look too many times in student days not to know what it presaged: "You always counseled an eye for the big chance," he hurriedly protested. "This is the big chance for me, and it requires finesse, diplomacy—not a bludgeon." The only reply was a dry crackling sound as the cellophane was stripped from Arnet's cigar. There was something ominous in Arnet's absorption in this irrelevant little action: Gray waited for the storm to break. . . . But for once he had misread his friend. Arnet was not aroused: he was confused. To him Gray's interruption had not been just a crude attempt at humor; it was a blunt indication that Gray was not taking his advice any longer. And he wondered if the relationship of pupil deferring to the professor, which had characterized all their years of friendship, had come to this abrupt and unpleasant end. . . . "Heading the research is not everything," he stated mildly. "You could make an excellent living out of a general practice."

Gray's head jerked about: he stared at Arnet as though he had not heard him correctly. But Arnet was placidly engaged in clipping the end from his cigar. Gray gave a short laugh: "You know, Hil, for a moment, I thought you had said that I could make an excellent living—"

"You heard me correctly."

Gray's face stiffened: "I must be laboring under an hallucination," he observed, and a slight tightness had come into his voice. "I thought you had me come to this hospital, *because of the opportunity to get the research foundation.*"

"I did: your research work with Curry and Stanton; your keen interest in arthritis— You were the logical man for the job." He shrugged. "The hospital thinks otherwise—why force the issue?"

"You know why—you know very well why."

Arnet shot a quick glance at him. Gray's face had gone deadly serious, the jaw set, the eyes filled with a brooding light. . . . That again! Gray's one blind spot: that obsession about making a dead man's dream a reality. . . . "Yes, I know why," agreed Arnet, "but face the facts: the opportunity for you in this hospital is closed—"

"It can be opened," maintained Gray. "I've found the key."

The fact that it was a devious sort of key did not seem to trouble him. He shrugged aside the deception he had to practise on a few people. Thousands would be helped by the cure his research would discover. Narrow minds would not grasp that a small evil was a negligible price for a great good. He had resigned himself to that fact when he had set his sights on achieving something important: "Isn't that the story of every great achievement: in spite of small minds it was pushed through to fulfilment?"

"And what will that do to you?"

Gray stared at him a long moment. "Didn't you cut any corners in your career, Hil?" he retorted, his voice significantly soft.

"Maybe I did," came the imperturbable reply. "And if I did—well, as you know, I advocate letting everyone make their own mistakes . . . but the price of some mistakes comes terribly high."

"If it's a mistake, it has been made already—and it has not affected me: I'm still the same."

"You are? There was a time when you did not neglect Elaine."

"Elaine?" Gray shot a surprised glance at his friend. "Has she been complaining to you?"

"She does not have to. . . . When a woman is with child she naturally expects more attention from her husband—" He broke off and looked at Gray significantly.

"What on earth are you driving at?" demanded Gray irritably.

"You wouldn't know," replied Arnet with heavy irony. "But I am talking about a Miss Sorrento."

"Sandra!" Honest amazement filled his countenance: "Why she doesn't mean a thing to me—not a thing—"

An incisive gesture cut short his protestations. Arnet did not want any rhetoric; he wanted an explanation. Why did Sandra hang with rapt absorption on his every word? What brought on the worshipful look in her eyes whenever she saw him? It was scarcely credible that she had arrived at this state of infatuation without some complicity on his part.

"You're seeing things," retorted Gray bluntly.

"Yes: unpleasant things—which a number of other people, too, are seeing and remarking."

Chagrined, Gray was forced into a reluctant explanation. Sandra had been on the verge of being expelled. At the staff meeting, held to determine the girl's fate, it had been plainly evident that the Mother Superioress and the Chief-of-Staff, Dr. Bromwell, *did not want her to be expelled.* She was their brand saved from the burning. They were hoping that someone would put in a good word for the girl, and so provide a reason for showing leniency. . . . "It was just the very kind of opening I had been looking for—I seized it."

Dr. Arnet's eyes were frosty. "And, thereby made yourself popular with the hospital by talking the girl into accepting the hospital's viewpoint."

Gray nodded: "It wasn't easy . . . and I still have to remind her, occasionally, when she goes off on a tangent. But she was allowed to graduate; she has her R.N. now, and, of course, she's grateful—that's all her behavior means." A smile quirked the corners of his mouth: "I'm grateful too—but I never let it show."

Dr. Arnet turned a distasteful look upon him, "And you still can't see?"

"See what?"

"What this is doing to you?"

"Are you back on that again?" He twisted away from him disgustedly. It angered him that the one man who knew the full scope and vast importance of this position for him, personally, should boggle over negligible minutiae: "How can you be so confoundedly obtuse, Hil?" he complained.

But Arnet was not obtuse: he saw very clearly. Gray was no longer just trying to fulfil a sacred trust: to win for his dead father's name the greatness which life had cheated him of— That might have been his original objective; but he had gone beyond that. Only one thing interested Gray now: to get to the top by any manner or means. . . . Arnet's voice was like a scalpel: "Individuals are not just inanimate pawns. . . . Use them that way and they will turn on you—and destroy you."

Sudden anger glinted in Gray's eyes, and his sharply cleft chin jutted forward threateningly. It took several moments before his hands released their tight hold of the wheel. His voice had a sharp edge to it:

"If I want my motives interpreted I'll go to an analyst—not to a friend." He flung up a hand forestalling Arnet's reply. "I know, I know—you spoke *because* you are a friend. . . . But it wasn't just friendship that made you make accusations like that—and you know it as well as I."

Dr. Arnet rapped out a sharp denial: but Gray countered quickly:

"Elaine and I are all the family you have . . . aren't we?" The irrelevancy of the remark caused Arnet to look blankly at him. "It is as plain as day," pursued Gray, "that the research is bound to lead to bigger things. Eventually, Elaine and I will have to go elsewhere—and you are going to be left alone."

With disconcerting adroitness Gray had reduced all Arnet's advice to selfish nothingness. For he did want Gray and Elaine near him. He needed them and their friendship. The arthritic condition which had started in his legs might reach his hands, and the dread of being completely dependent on the soulless ministrations of hired help was an ever-present possibility. . . .

Gray's eyes coolly appraised his discomfiture: "Why not be honest," he suggested, "and admit it?"

"Honest?" For a moment indignation choked him. "You tell me to be honest . . . after what you are doing . . . every day . . . in the hospital?"

41

"What I am doing is just a logical carrying out of the things you taught me."

The thin cheeks of Dr. Arnet reddened with anger. "I taught you to face the evidence of your senses," he snapped, "not to hide behind hypocrisy."

Gray glanced up at his friend's angry face: "There is not much sense in losing our tempers over this, Hil. We see eye to eye on principles—this is just a difference of opinion about procedures."

"Procedures!" Arnet mouthed the word angrily. "Don't try to cover up facts with words. What you are doing is just as dangerous as a faulty operation. You can close up the incision with perfect suturing, but the sickness is still there . . . inside . . . and unless it is corrected, your patient dies."

Gray coolly dismissed the comparison: he had seen to it that every move was carefully calculated and executed. The margin of error had been reduced to practically nothing: "I've made a very thorough study of this hospital. I know just how it functions and why. . . ."

Bluntly, Arnet retorted that Gray did not know what he was talking about. Only an utter fool, he added, would imagine that he had grasped the complexities of this institution's beliefs. Did he, for one instant, flatter himself that he had solved the riddle of the chaplain's personality? His bewildering idealisms, mystic compulsions, and strivings?

"I've done that already." The matter-of-fact statement caused Arnet's mouth to drop open in surprise. "It was not very difficult," Gray assured him. "He wrote a book: I read it. Afterwards I went to him and asked questions. He spent hours making everything clear to me. . . . I know more about this hospital's beliefs than the people who run it." He flicked a challenging glance at Arnet. "Want to try me out on it?"

Arnet muttered something that sounded like "that would prove nothing." The cool audacity of what Gray had done left him dazed: he could not for the moment think of anything to say in reply.

The dim light from the dashboard emphasized the expression on Arnet's countenance. There was no reason, Gray decided, for this open resentment. A man had to be a totally impervious little world of his own in order to achieve fulfilment. . . . Arnet had always inculcated that. Why did he now show resentment when the pupil acted on the advice of the master?

"It won't work. . . . I still say it won't work." Determination had brought Arnet's head upright, the dogged determination of a man so used to being right that he cannot yield, even though the proofs of his wrongness are staring him in the face. "They won't give it to you," he declared stubbornly. "I know they won't." His voice rose slightly. "Mark my words: you are not going to head this research foundation."

The sound of the whirring rubber tires on concrete made a dim ominous accompaniment to his prophetic words.

When Gray finally spoke, a faint tinge of malice had come into his voice: "I am terribly sorry, Hil, if this upsets you," he said, "but . . . *I am in charge of the research foundation.* Dr. Bromwell appointed me yesterday."

For a long moment there was complete silence in the car, then Arnet turned away and stared blindly out into the gathering dusk. Anger flamed hot in him at having been led on like this— But as swiftly as his anger had come, it was gone, swallowed up by another emotion, one that was new, and because of its very newness, frightening. His judgment had been wrong, completely wrong! And it was a bitter and terrible thing to have his self-assurance stripped from him by the very one whose own self-assurance was the product of his teaching. . . .

There was a slight jar as the car came to a halt. Gray leaned forward and extracted the keys from the ignition. His hand came down lightly, almost patronizingly on his friend's shoulder. Arnet turned; there was still that smile on Gray's face. "We have arrived," Gray said.

Dr. Arnet became aware of the hospital entrance and the shadows of evening deep about the building. He got out of the car slowly, almost with that strange carefulness that one sees in the old who know their importance to others is ended.

They entered the lobby, and, with the mechanicalness of daily habit, Dr. Arnet went over to the in-and-out board. The little peg before his name said "Out." He put a finger on it, and, as he did, a voice spoke in back of him, "Congratulations, doctor." He spun about: it was Sister Felicita, the day-receptionist, smiling brightly up at Gray.

Stiffly Dr. Arnet stalked past them out of the room, and

Gray was saying smoothly, ". . . the first to congratulate me, Sister. . . . I appreciate that a great deal."

Admiration shone brightly in the Sister's eyes: "Everyone thinks it's wonderful that you were selected, doctor—it's such an important responsibility."

"It is—and I could use some help." He pointed at the rosary hanging from her belt. "May I depend on you?"

"You certainly may, doctor," she assured him. "All the Sisters will be praying for you."

"I think," he said with a pleased smile, "the research foundation is going to be a success."

As he walked away Sister Felicita's admiring glance followed him. Somehow, whenever he entered the office, he brought an air of importance, of assurance, with him; and after he left there would come over her a feeling of discontent because of the smallness and insignificance of the tasks assigned her.

Tiredly, she sat down at her desk. It had been a very demanding day. She stared a moment at the tightly filled file of cards. This was her life and her love: a box of cards, exactly made out, neatly inscribed. Each day new cards were made out, old ones withdrawn. It was an unending ebb and flow of life, its joy and sorrow and pain. . . .

From the opposite corner of the room the muted voice of the switchboard operator seemed infinitely remote: "St. Luke's Hospital. . . . Yes?—One moment, please." The small quiet sound of a connection clicked home. . . .

Sister Felicita sighed gently. In her novitiate days she had

visioned herself as a ministering angel among the stricken.
How eagerly she had entered the halls of this hospital, ready
for long vigils with the sick, for patient ministration to pain!
Instead they had assigned her to this desk, with its box of
cards and its treadmill duties. By slow steps, she had come
to the conclusion that things were never, in reality, as we
dream them to be. And yet that conviction held no bitterness
nor disillusionment. For to live was to love, and loving was
doing, not dreaming. The hospital was a complicated estab-
lishment, and the functioning of all its departments was co-
ordinated by the little collection of cards which she held
beneath her hand. She touched her fingers to them again,
lightly, smilingly. . . .

Footsteps sounded heavily in the corridor at the end of
the lobby, but she did not lift her head. It was a familiar
sound, heavy, crowded, as of many people walking. There
was a rhythm to the footsteps, not the strictly cadenced one
of marching men, yet holding a semblance to that ordered
sound. Casually, she lifted her eyes. The night shift was
coming on duty. She could see them go past: young girls,
trim in their starched uniforms, well rested, intelligent-eyed.
In the morning, they would again go down that same corridor: weariedly, worn out from their night-long watch by
the side of the sick; thinking only of rest and sleep. But now
they walked briskly, as though there were nothing more
desirable than menial service for the sick and suffering. . . .

Sister Martha, the plump-faced, dimple-cheeked night receptionist, came up to the side of her desk: "Have you heard

the news"—she was slightly breathless with suppressed excitement—"about Dr. Powers? He has been appointed—"

"Isn't it wonderful?"

"Wonderful? It's awful— Don't look so shocked. You would feel the same way if you had the night shift. I just dread the idea of him leaving. Everything has gone so smoothly since he has been resident—"

"I know, Sister, I know. If only we had more like him!" She gave a little sigh. "Well"—with a gesture she indicated some papers on the desk—"here is the data on today's arrivals."

Sister Martha leaned forward to scan the reports. She ran a finger between her plump cheek and the tight edge of her coif. "Feels warm in here," she murmured. "Was the air-conditioning on today?" Without waiting for a reply, she ran on with some questions about one of the patients, jotting down memoranda all the while.

The voice of the telephone operator took on a brisker tone as lights began flashing with increasing frequency on the switchboard. . . .

Sister Felicita did some things to her veil, unpinned from her cuff a scrap of paper bearing some notes, then bade Sister Martha good night.

With no halt or jar, with the smoothness of well-meshed gears, the hospital ended its day, and its night of service had begun. . . .

Chapter 5

THE word of Gray's appointment contained a magic all its own: suddenly everyone was aware of him. As he threaded his way down the corridors, nurses, orderlies, Sisters stopped to greet and congratulate him. Even doctors, who formerly had had only a perfunctory nod for him, seemed to have developed an immediate need for a word of advice from him: about one of their patients; about a certain type of surgical technique or medication. . . .

He found their attention very satisfying. Coming as it did hard on the heels of his encounter with Arnet, this sudden show of attention was vindication of everything he had told his friend. All these people individually were negligible, but the sum total of their corporate opinion had been extremely important. Impressed by his behavior, their good opinion had communicated itself to the ones in authority. . . . His painstaking campaign had paid off—and no one was the worse for it.

Dr. Reynolds tried to halt him for a few minutes of small talk, but he brushed him expansively aside. "Headquarters, Ralph," he explained. "The Chief-of-Staff awaits," and with a smile he continued on his way.

Tonight would be his last stint of duty as a resident, and, from then on, Ralph and a number of other people were going to find him difficult of approach. . . . Sandra, he decided (because of the unrestraint Arnet had noticed in her) fell in that category—her usefulness was ended.

The black-cassocked figure of the chaplain was standing before a door. . . . With cynical eyes Gray watched the priest hesitate, square his shoulders, then enter the room. "I wonder," he thought with a smile, "what Arnet would have thought of *that!*"

Secretly, this play-acting of the chaplain always irritated him, but tonight he could find nothing but amusement in this childish attempt to attract attention. . . .

Dr. Bromwell was seated at his desk when he entered the office. He was a bald-headed, bespectacled bulk of a man, the stout face a grayish monotone of flesh out of which jutted an incongruous thin beak of a nose. His coat looked as though he had slept in it. Certainly, personal appearance had not got him his position as Chief-of-Staff. . . .

He gestured Gray to a chair: "Sorry to bother you, doctor, but there is a patient who came in this morning"—he picked up a card on which were scribbled some notes—"a Mr. Clayton, an arthritic. . . . Would you want to take care of him as part of the research project?"

The phrasing of the request (for it was a request and not an order) pleased Gray. Subtly yet surely it established the new relationship between them: in the future they would meet and confer as equals. Yet he had to demur. The research foundation was not as yet ready to handle patients.

Dr. Bromwell brushed that objection aside as a matter that could be speedily remedied if Gray was willing to handle the man's case. He had, along with the arthritic condition, a malignancy of the lungs, in an advanced stage.

Gray frowned thoughtfully. Medically they could do little for the man; and research would profit nothing from caring for him. "If you can arrange a room for him," he decided, "we will take care of him."

"He's not exactly an easy patient," warned Dr. Bromwell, "he has had so much suffering that—"

"The man is sick," Gray broke in. "That's all that is necessary. I'll do the best I can for him, doctor."

Dr. Bromwell's pudgy face was suddenly very benign. "I like that kind of attitude in a medical man."

Gray's cheeks reddened at the open praise. "My own father died from a malignancy of the lungs—" His lips closed suddenly as though the words had slipped out unaware.

"Oh?" Concern replaced the pleased look in Bromwell's

countenance. "I didn't know." His lips puffed in and out, contemplatively. "If this case would be bound up too much with painful memories—"

But Gray would not accept the escape so considerately offered. He wanted to take care of Clayton. The doctor and nurses who had taken care of his father had been so generous and kind that, well, it had put a sort of obligation on him.

There was only a slight elevation of Bromwell's eyebrows to show that he had heard and understood. Gray got to his feet: "I'll get right on with it," he promised.

"Just a moment, doctor. There is another matter." Gray stood still. "You will have to continue as resident for a little while. . . ."

Chagrined, Gray listened to the rest of it: the acute shortage of doctors, the arrangement for a Dr. Lawrence to take over for him each night at midnight. . . .

The sharpness of his annoyance was all out of proportion to this small disagreeableness. And he realized why that was so. It was not so much because this stupid arrangement slighted the importance of the research by placing it on the level with the chores of the residency, but because it compelled him to keep on giving lip-service to the hospital's ideals for some additional days. That irked him: but he could not do anything about it. He needed the good will and support of the Chief-of-Staff until the research work was fully functioning—

At the second floor desk Gray stopped to report that he was in charge of the Clayton case.

The head nurse made no secret of her relief: she had just been about to call the main desk for a doctor; Miss Sorrento, who was specialing Clayton, had reported him to be in a state of deep depression . . . completely apathetic.

"Has he been having plenty of liquids?"

She assured him that he had. "We have been watching that carefully, doctor, because of all the sedation."

"Probably something psychologic then," he decided. "I had better have a look at him."

Sandra opened the door, her features primly composed; but at sight of him a radiant smile dissolved every vestige of her prim politeness. For a significant second he faced her, his face an expressionless blank; and then: "I'll be a little while, nurse," he said briskly, and his head moved in a slight gesture of command. "Wait outside."

The smile seemed to congeal on her face; and without a word, she went past him, out of the room, closing the door in back of her. She stood there, in the emptiness of the corridor, her lips moving, silently framing the curt order he had spoken to her: "Wait outside, nurse." Nurse! That was all she was to him. Someone to do his bidding. Someone to be treated as a human being only when they were alone, when no one could see them—for the rest of the time she was just a cypher, a puppet, a thing of no feelings, inanimate, except when he pulled the strings. . . . Did he think he could treat her like that? She would make him aware of her . . . as a person. She would make him want her—her attention, her smile. Some way or other, she would—

The vehemence of her passionate resolve sent a trembling all through her. It shocked her into sudden remembrance: she had promised him there would be no more of this. Was she forgetting already? . . . These past days had been so peaceful, so satisfying: she had been living in his world, the kind of world in which he dwelt. . . . She must not lose it . . . she must not . . . she would not. . . .

A surgical cart moved past her. . . . The doctor, walking beside it, was talking in a loud brash way, totally oblivious that there were doors standing open and people present. The two elderly nurses accompanying him, nodded attentively, respectfully, to his directions, their faces giving no hint of their true feelings. . . .

Sandra's attention came suddenly into sharp focus. She watched them, marveling at the self-control of the nurses. This particular surgeon was well known and abominated for his caustic tongue, his flaming impatience; and yet these two nurses—

It burst on her like an inspiration. This was what Gray had wanted to point out to her: *the individual had to be submerged when caring for others; doctors and nurses, when on duty, had to act professionally.* . . .

Of course, she knew that (it had been dinned into her during her years of training), but her feeling for him must have been showing too openly, and so he had taken the quick and ready way to warn her. "He could have done it differently though," she complained; but then it was his way to be direct. In any event that was of small consequence compared to the underlying significance of his behavior: for it was evident to her that Gray must be aware that there was *another relationship between them,* a relationship which had to be subordinated when they worked together as doctor and nurse. . . .

And suddenly everything was right again, wondrously right, and extremely simple: she had only to follow his lead, dutifully, on the ascending road he walked. . . .

Intently Gray stared at the inert man. Gaunt cheeks, wasted flesh were all that were left of what must have once been a tall strong body. . . . Memories crowded up in him—far-off memories—of the one whom he had loved with childhood's devastating completeness; the one whom he had seen wasting away before his eyes while he was powerless to help. . . . Those days and weeks were etched undyingly in his heart, forming memories that he could never get rid of, no matter how hard he tried. . . .

Unwonted gentleness came into his voice: "Mr. Clayton?" (The face was a torpid mask.) "I am Dr. Powers . . . in charge of you now—" Out of the eyes looked complete hopelessness.

Gray sat down at the bedside and began to talk: he wheedled; he sympathized; he threatened—and suddenly, tears brimmed the man's eyes and ran sluggishly down his cheeks. They seemed not to be the tears of the living; they pushed their way out like drops of water pressed from a dead sponge.

Gray waited, but the man said nothing. Out of the drab emptiness of the face stared the mindless eyes like bits of polished gray glass. His father's eyes had been that same light gray color, and the last time those eyes had looked at him— He spun about and walked away from the bed. The window stood open, and lights were coming on in the distant town: beads of light joined by links of darkness. Beads . . . darkness . . . and death—

Death! . . . The thought of it was like a ponderous hand closing down on his mind; a vast blackness that was nothingness. It was real and it was present, here, in this room, brooding over that man in the bed, enveloping him— Angrily he shook himself free of the somber thought. *Life* stretched out before him, the fullness of life. Did not his newly won position as head of the research bring with it the best that life could offer—financial security, prominence, achievement? Why then this sudden and morbid mood about death? It could only be the result of some chance association of ideas. . . . The beads! Of course, that was it! He had never quite rid his mind of the strange impression Joyce had made that night when she explained to him what the praying of her rosary could do for her. It had been fantastic: the absolute faith, although death was so devastatingly near; the total trust, in a string of beads, when it was he alone who stood between her and death. . . . Momentarily he felt again the vast pity that had seized him then, and he knew that although the others (Sandra, Ralph, and the rest) would be brushed aside, he could not desert Joyce. He could not, he told himself, let her be victimized by her pathetic childish beliefs—

A low moan wavered through the darkening room. He

turned. The eyes of the man on the bed were lifted to the opposite wall; a crucifix hung there. Tears were spilling slowly down the man's cheeks, and his lips were twisted as though in an atempt to speak. . . .

"Does it bother you?" Gray asked. "I'll take it down, if you want."

The man came upright in bed, his face a torture of pleading, his hands clutched at his throat. . . .

Gray crossed the room, reached up and unfastened the crucifix.

There was a sound as the door of the room swung open. Over his shoulder Gray glimpsed Father Chriswell, standing inside the door. Vaguely embarrassed, Gray stared at him a moment; then, as though realizing the stupidity of attempting a retreat, he turned fully and, with a show of decision, placed the crucifix on the table.

The priest came forward: "Did I interrupt something, doctor?"

"No, not exactly, Father." He pointed a finger at the crucifix. "It seemed to be bothering the patient."

The priest reached out and touched it, nodding slowly. "It is a bothersome thing," he agreed. "For some it makes no sense, and for others it speaks too clearly."

A thick clotted rasp of sound broke from the sick man's throat: "Take that thing out of here!" he demanded.

Father Chriswell turned: the face of Clayton was no longer blank. Anger had swept the mistiness from his eyes and brought determination into every line of the cadaverous countenance.

"Why?" asked the priest, and his voice was very gentle: "Why should we take it away?"

"I got enough pain of my own. I don't want to be looking at His."

The priest's eyes met the patient's quietly. "Even if, by looking at His, you will be healed?"

The look of outraged amazement and unbelief that came into the man's eyes was something Gray could very well understand. His own amazement, when first he had heard that fantastic idea expressed, was still startlingly vivid. He had read it in the chaplain's book—that fatuous book, which had so tragically influenced Joyce. . . . But Clayton was a different proposition! The man's gaze—a hard, demanding challenge—was turned now on him. Gray met it, directly . . . and something intangible, and yet very real, seemed to pass between them . . . something that linked them together secretly and surely against this stiff figure in black opposing them.

Clayton was fumbling back the sleeve of his pajama coat: "Look at that: skin and bones. . . ." He stabbed a bony finger towards the cross: "How is *that* . . . going to heal this?" The priest was silent. "I'm waiting," he pressed. "Why don't you tell me? Can't you find the words?"

"Yes, I can find the words," came the meek response, "but I don't know if you will listen to them."

"I'll listen. Go ahead. I'm listening."

The priest fixed his gaze upon the man: " 'Unless you take up your cross and follow me—you are not worthy of me.' "

Disappointment wrenched the sick man's mouth into a

twisted line of bitterness. "That!" he said, and a feeble wave of the hand dismissed it. "I heard that before."

"Most people have." There was no change in the equable voice. "Do you know what it means?" Clayton's eyes had closed in weary disgust. "Do you?" insisted the priest.

The sick man muttered assent: he knew what it meant. Slowly his eyes opened. "But what good is it going to do me to act like He did? Why should I put my arms around this . . . this curse of humanity."

"It isn't just a curse," denied the priest mildly. "It's also a challenge: to be like Him."

"He's dead."

"But He lives—"

"In heaven," broke in the man sarcastically.

"Not only there, also here. He lives on . . . in every man who suffers with Him and like Him . . . and so shares in His greatness."

"Greatness?" He gave a short bitter laugh. "What was His greatness? He suffered just like the rest of us."

"He forgave the ones who hurt him."

Dumfounded, the man stared at Him: "Is that your idea of greatness? That was weakness," he grated harshly.

The priest shook his head firmly in dissent. "You don't mean that. You know you don't." He pointed out that everyone (even brute animals) had the instinct and ability to attack the one who hurts them. To forgive required more than a natural power. "In fact you can't do it alone—you're just a human being. There is something divine in being able to forgive deliberately inflicted pain."

Weariedly the man turned his head on the pillow. "Who wants to be divine? All I want is to be alive, to be healthy, happy. Is that asking too much? Other people don't have what I've got. Why do I have to have it?" His voice rose: "I hate pain. I hate it and I always will."

"So do I."

The quiet words of agreement seemed to hang in the silence of the room. The man in the bed looked stupidly at the priest for a moment: "What was that?" he finally ventured. "What did you say?"

"I said I hate pain."

"I thought you were a man of God—and you *hate* pain?"

"That's why I hate it: God hates it."

"*He* hates it?"

"In itself it is evil. He has to hate it."

"Why did He make it then?"

The priest's voice was patient, unruffled. "He didn't make it. Pain is not a creation," he explained, "it's a negation, an absence of something. . . ." He hesitated. There was so much to be told; and it reached so far back into the mysterious depths of mankind's original tragedy. . . . To uncover those truths to a mind untouched by faith, cynical, darkened . . . and yet, faith came by hearing. He spoke slowly: "We were made free, and, freely we chose to abandon Him, to go our own way, along a road that seemed bright, and was in reality dark. . . . Maybe it is necessary that, to come back to Him, we have to take *His* way, a road that seems dark, and is in reality bright."

"Maybe, maybe. . . . Tell me why and not maybe."

Mildly the deep-set eyes of the priest met the sick man's: "Don't you allow a doctor to cut in order to cure you?"

"Of course, because it makes sense. What you're saying doesn't."

"Nothing does—until you give it a fair trial."

The drooping shoulders of the sick man seemed to stiffen slightly against the pillows. He had been challenged: and the chaplain would not have thrown down the gauntlet unless he was sure. . . . A light flickered fitfully in Clayton's eyes, and then abruptly a despairing hopelessness quenched it: "I've tried everything," he remembered bitterly, "and nothing worked. Since I've been sick I've tried everything they had on the market . . . and nothing helped. I'm not cured. I'm worse. . . ."

Hesitantly, almost hopefully, he lifted his eyes, but the priest's attention had left him. His gaze seemed riveted on the table at the side of the bed: but there was nothing there to warrant this strange absorption . . . only an empty glass, and a pitcher filled to the brim with water. . . .

When the priest finally looked at him again, it was with eyes that were fathomless pools of pity. "The truth," he assured him, "never fails . . . and the truth is: you come to God on your knees, or not at all—" He drew a deep breath, and slowly his expression altered and the dark eyes kindled; his voice cut cleanly through the silence of the room, urgent and sure: "There is a purpose in what has happened to you— there has to be. Fighting it, the way an animal does, lowers you to that level. . . . Using it lifts you to greatness—

makes the curse into a blessing. . . . You once knew a great truth and have forgotten it: you don't live by bread alone; you are body and soul—a unit; and if you live only by your body then only half of you lives. I'm asking you to fully live —because that full living embraces and gives meaning to everything that happens to you, even sickness, suffering, and death. . . ."

The deep driving sincerity of the pleading voice laid a spell upon the room; and under its influence, the tortured look was fading from the sick man's eyes, the grim lines about the mouth softening, making him strangely different . . . peaceful. . . .

In the background Gray's broad shoulders bulked solidly large and real. The broad planes of his face were as smooth and hard as the polished facets of a cut stone. Coldly, analytically, he had followed Father Chriswell's reasoning down to the last impassioned word. And now, with one thrust, he would puncture the whole inflated fairy-tale. His teeth gritted together sharply, as, on the verge of speech, he remembered— He could not speak: to expose the chaplain's falsehood would expose his own!

The eyes of the sick man had wavered away from Father Chriswell and were turned to him. There was stark pleading in the depths of those gray eyes, a sort of bewildered appeal. Clayton wanted *him* to agree with the chaplain!

Anger flared up in him; anger at this mad apostle who preached a gospel he had never practised; anger because he had been forced into this precarious position.

Clayton was speaking, urging him to advise him—and Father Chriswell had turned and was looking at him, waiting for him to speak. He had to answer; somehow he had to make an answer. He drew a deep breath, and his voice sounded husky and unreal in his own ears: "You have nothing to lose," he said, spacing his words carefully, "and everything to gain."

The words could only be taken for agreement; but somehow, with that uncanny intuitiveness the sick sometimes have, Clayton sensed Gray's true feelings. His voice had a tinge of apology: "When you are as far gone as I am you'll try anything . . . anything." Then turning towards the priest: "But I can't go for this completely . . . not yet . . . I've got to talk it out . . . a lot more. . . ."

Sudden relief swept through Gray. Clayton was not completely deceived; but he would be, if exposed to any more of the chaplain's specious reasoning: "I think you ought to rest now, Mr. Clayton," he counseled. "You have done enough talking for one day."

But Clayton stubbornly decided he wanted to talk: he had to find out; this was not something that could wait.

He did not see Gray's sudden sharp glance of warning. One wasted hand had already lifted and was pointing at the cross: "You can put that back, Father . . . where it was before. . . ."

Father Chriswell took it and put it back in its place, on the wall opposite the bed.

Chapter 6

WITH short, hurried steps, Gray stalked away from the room. A nurse went past him, and he was aware that she had stopped and turned to stare at him, wondering, doubtless, what vital emergency was occasioning his unusual haste. But he did not moderate his pace. The inability to voice his true feelings had left him like a coiled spring. . . . A slight shiver of apprehension went through him when he thought how closely he had come to disaster. The insane urge to demolish the chaplain's sophistries had almost been his undoing. It would have taken only one wrong word, one rash sentence. . . .

A sense of painful constriction stole up through his hands.

He looked down at them. They were tightly knotted into fists at his side. Angrily he unflexed them and thrust them into his pockets. . . .

He had never dreamed that a routine call on a patient would prove as upsetting as this. But then he had only himself to blame. Freely, he had taken Clayton's case, with no intention of impressing Dr. Bromwell. The reasons he had given the Chief-of-Staff had been honest reasons. He had acted impulsively. It had been a mistake.

The whole thing had been a mistake. It always was a mistake to think with your heart instead of your head. You wound up by being taken advantage of. That was what had happened to his father . . . and, long ago, he had promised himself not to make the same error. But he had—

Yet, as the first flush of anger abated, he realized that the unpleasant incident might have its recompense. For he had seen, at first hand, what an insidious web the chaplain could weave. It never did to underrate an opponent. What was it that Arnet had had to say about the man? It had been some kind of warning: maybe old Hil had known what he was talking about. Certainly, the chaplain had come off best in this engagement . . . but when next they met it would be under circumstances of his own choosing—and the gloves would be off. . . .

But that did not wholly remove the sting of having so badly underestimated the man. How could he have been so obtuse as to think his eccentric behavior just the silly posturings of a vain man! It was the carefully contrived plan of campaign of a person who wanted to dominate the lives of others. He was a menace, a walking lie. . . . The effrontery of the man! To go around telling people that pain could be used! . . . That it could be turned into a blessing— Well, maybe it could be used; maybe it could be a blessing—for those who professionally cared and cured the sick. They got paid for it. That was as far as the chaplain's ideas had any validity. Beyond that they were just so much claptrap. . . . Up till now he had been content to let him enjoy his little world of make-believe, but this incident changed everything. The shabby trick the priest had played on him, in forcing him to agree with his views, rankled. It was something that had to be undone, at the first possible chance—and he promised himself that when the time came he would do it, with a devastating thoroughness. . . .

The head nurse was not at the chart desk, but Sandra was.

At sight of him she stood up quickly, her whole expression and bearing a model of ready, respectful attention.

"The Clayton chart, please," he requested.

She placed it before him, and he sat down and began to write. She stood to one side, slightly in back of him. Her dark gaze went lingeringly over the firm flesh of his cheek, the hard clean line of jaw and chin, the wavy mass of black hair swept from the brow—it was abundantly thick and glossy— and for one blind breathless moment she wanted to stretch forth her hand and touch it with the tips of her fingers, softly, caressingly.

He moved suddenly, thrusting the pen into its holder. She stepped farther back, aware of the sudden warmth that had come into her cheeks. And then after an uncomfortable pause: "Are there any instructions, doctor?" she murmured.

He did not look up: "It's all down here." His finger tapped the chart: "The sedation continues, as indicated." He reached forward and took up the pen again. "He has come out of the apathy. . . . You may go back on duty." He heard her as she turned to leave. "Just a moment! The chaplain is still with him."

With one quick step she was at his side, her face radiant; "Oh, I felt sure he would help him!"

There was no mistaking the elated look in her eyes: she was expecting commendation for what she had done! The meddlesome impertinence of the girl, presuming to call in the chaplain before consulting him. He could not trust himself to speak.

Abruptly he turned his back on her, picked up the chart, and made a pretense of checking the instructions he had just written. He drew it out interminably, letting her sense the full weight of his displeasure. Finally he spoke to her, over his shoulder: "Wait outside the patient's door," he ordered, "until the chaplain leaves."

She went away, her retreating footsteps making a small, forlorn sound in the long, empty corridor.

Chapter 7

WITH a grateful little sigh, Father Chriswell lowered himself into his easy chair. It was past his bedtime, and he should not be sitting here like this. Guiltily he looked at the open door. Perhaps he should get up and close it. Sister Mildred, he thought to himself, will scold if she comes by and sees that door open. But the support of the chair's cushions felt so good against his tired back—and he did not agree with the good Sister's ideas anyhow. Office hours, he stubbornly maintained, were not for a hospital chaplain. And just now, nothing was quite so important as the strange things that had happened in Clayton's room. . . .

It was amazing (now that the incident was ended) what

startling parallels and epigrammatic replies kept thronging through his mind. "It seems," he muttered wryly to himself, "I am in the nature of being a delayed-action bomb—the brilliant rejoinders come *after* everything is over."

He decided that all the years spent in lecturing from prepared notes was the cause of this. "My mental reflexes are rusted . . . or maybe this ability to think on your feet is a special gift, one that I've never had." He made a mental note to pray for it; the episode in the sick man's room showed he had urgent need of it.

How inept his replies to Clayton had been—and yet, the man had been touched. . . . He shook his head in bewilderment. The man's cynical opposition had frightened him: it had been like an unyielding wall. Yet, after all his futile words were spoken and when hope was almost dead, an unseen Hand, as it were, had reached forth—and the unyielding wall began to give way.

The wonder of it was still on him: a bright little flame of joy cupped shelteringly in the hands of his humble gratitude. For he did not deceive himself. What had been effected through him had been effected *in spite of him*. Startling as the result was, even more startling and complete it might have been if he had been more fully what he was supposed to be. . . .

His evening tray still stood on a table. The food had gone cold. He took a glass of milk, sipped it, then put it down. He crossed the room, entered his bedroom and pressed the call bell. A nurse came and took away the tray.

He went back into the bedroom and took off his cincture

and cassock. With practised ease, his fingers found and undid the fastenings that held the complicated brace supporting his back. . . . For a moment he stood there, his shoulders slumped forward, all the rigidity gone from his bearing.

Abruptly he sat down, his hands bracing against the edge of the bed . . . waiting for the sudden wave of pain to pass. But it clung to him, like a malignant flame, twisting his lips, sealing his eyes, losing him, for the moment, in its dark embrace. . . .

The words of consolation and help which he had for others, he never could find for himself—not when pain was upon him. Then he knew only one thing: that he hated it, and yet wanted it. For he could never lose sight of its power and greatness.

He lifted his head and stared about him, as though seeking assistance. . . . There, on his bedside table, it was: a small, cardboard box, with a label affixed: "Two tablets as needed for pain." Somberly he stared at it, remembering the things he had written, the things he had seen lived out by a frail, small child of a woman.

Shame crept through every part of him: the hidden shame that had haunted so many years of his life. While other priests spent their days and nights in the exhausting activities of apostolic work, he had sat comfortably in a professor's chair. All his life he had wanted to be one of the doers—and all his life he had been only a talker, a writer. And now, when the chance had come to do the work which he had always craved, he found his body unfit to meet the demands made upon it. . . .

That was not important. God had got most done when He did nothing. He had helped us most when most helpless— on the cross! And, mysteriously enough, man, too, if he wished, could re-live the mystery of the cross—he, too, could help others most when most helpless. . . .

He was thinking of Clayton as he came to his feet: the ravaged face, the gray eyes bewildered with suffering; the thrusting, demanding questions, masking the fear and hopelessness in his heart. . . . He was still thinking of him as his hand closed about the little box, and, with the carefully slow steps of an old man, made his way into his study, dropped the box into a drawer and doggedly shut it. . . .

Unmindful of the open door, he shuffled towards the prie-dieu and knelt down. The open pages of his breviary stared up at him, the words meaningless, like a sightless face. He could not pray, could not read. He hid his face in his hands. . . .

Like a living, angry thing, pain spread wide through his back and shoulders. His face contorted, half-finished words of prayer breathed from his lips; he moved from one knee to the other, rocking from side to side in a rhythm of hopelessness, repeating his act of acceptance—but it was a dim, unfeeling acceptance . . . buried in the depths of his will . . . beyond words or feeling . . . because the pain was everything. . . .

He lifted his gaze. Above him hung the crucifix— When they challenged Him, he did not come down from the cross; and he— Abjectly, his chin came down against his chest:

"Have pity on my weakness," he begged humbly, ". . . have pity. . . ."

For a long time he knelt there, unmoving, until he could stand it no longer. Slowly he came to his feet and went to the desk. With fingers that no longer had any feeling, he was trying to fumble open the drawer when the dry, sharp sound of a rap startled him. He straightened up and turned; but the invitation to enter died on his lips.

Dr. Bromwell stood on the threshold: "The door was open," he said, and there was reproof, not apology, in his voice. "I merely knocked to let you know I was here—" He broke off, and his spectacles seemed suddenly two pitilessly inquiring circlets of glass:

"Your back is acting up again, isn't it?" he accused, and, without giving him time to reply: "I'm not asking you if you took them—where are they?"

"Here; right in my hand," replied Father Chriswell opening his hand. "I was just about to take them." He met the doctor's disbelieving stare. "Really I was."

Dr. Bromwell tossed his hat on a chair, took the box, placed two tablets in the priest's hand, got a glass of water and stood over him: "Take them—*now*."

Obediently the priest swallowed them. He looked up at the doctor and attempted a placating smile—but Dr. Bromwell was not being placated. He stalked over to the window and glared unseeingly into the dark outside. From his pocket he had pulled his watch and now he started winding it, rapidly, energetically. There was a sudden click, and from inside the

71

watch a curious whirring flurry of sound that lasted a brief moment and then ended. . . . He stared at it—another mainspring . . . the second one this week! Some day he was going to let the chaplain know how many mainsprings he was costing him. . . . His barrel-like chest rose in a prodigious sigh. What on earth did one do with a patient like this? Vicarious suffering, reparation—he knew what these things were, and he believed in them. But he was a doctor, not a spiritual director; and a doctor's job was to cure, or, failing that, to control the effects of a disease as much as possible. Father Chriswell would have plenty of suffering in spite of all medical assistance—maybe saints should be left to go their own way. . . . He shrugged. He did not know the right procedure in handling saints, but he did know how to handle patients—

The useless watch was thrust into his pocket as he walked over to the desk: "Feeling better?" The priest nodded. Dr. Bromwell picked up his hat, studied it a moment, then fixed the priest with a stern glance: "There is not much sense in me prescribing for you, if you don't take the medicine . . . is there?" Father Chriswell's head was bowed penitently. "You're supposed to set the example here—"

The chaplain's head lifted: "They say priests make bad patients," he offered.

"And is that a virtue?"

He admitted, reluctantly, that it was not.

"Then don't glory in it."

The retort silenced him for a moment; then in a voice of

72

childlike candor: "I'll do better from now on, doctor," he assured him.

The thin brows of Dr. Bromwell went upwards skeptically. "I hope that means what I think it does . . . and not that you are going to take precautions *so that I don't walk in on you again.*"

"I never lock my door," protested Father Chriswell.

"Everyone knows that . . . and maybe that's why your back is giving you so much trouble."

"But a chaplain should be available at all times, doctor."

Dr. Bromwell sighed. "You are—but, if you keep this up, before long you won't be available at all."

Chapter 8

TIME, which moves so slowly for those awaiting some great fulfilment, moved twice as slowly for Gray whose highest expectation had been fulfilled. The ambiguous position resulting from Dr. Bromwell's stupid lack of foresight was the cause of this anomaly. Each day was an oppressive burden. Sandra, the chaplain, Reynolds were people who no longer had any relation to him, no significance. Yet he was forced to meet them, work with them, speak to them—and the burden of it was a dead weight that he was forced to carry. . . .

There were two post-operative cases on his list, he noted, as he started his rounds. The evening visiting hour was not yet over, but the corridors seemed strangely empty. He felt vaguely uneasy: he had noticed this sensation before, and he wondered what there was about a long empty corridor that brought on this formless disquiet. He had tramped the length of enough hospital corridors in his career—they could hold nothing new for him.

The head nurse was on the phone as he came up to the desk and she held the receiver out towards him: "For you, doctor," she said.

It was Dr. Bromwell, exuding satisfaction: "Some of the equipment has come in," he announced importantly. "Will you be able to check it tomorrow? Have you assistants—"

There was a trace of officiousness here that gave Gray the opening for what he wanted to say. He had, of course, already hired competent assistants, and they would be on hand to assist him. "But you must realize," he added, "that from now on the demands on my time will be considerably increased. It is imperative that you engage some doctor to replace me in the residency as soon as—"

The head nurse was tapping him lightly on the shoulder and gesturing upwards, as though trying to call his attention to something. With a curt gesture he cut her off. Bromwell was making apologies: there were several prospective candidates for the position; they would be here for an interview— in a few days!

The receiver rattled angrily into place. He turned to the head nurse. "Now, what was it you were trying to tell me, nurse?"

A slight tinge of color came into her cheeks. "I'm sorry to

have disturbed you, doctor," she said primly, "but the intercom was paging you. You are wanted in the emergency room."

"Accident?"

"It . . . it doesn't seem so," she said, and her cheeks were now plainly red.

"Is it a man . . . woman . . . child . . . ?"

"A woman—unconscious." He waited, while she inwardly berated herself for neglecting to get the necessary details instead of bothering him while on the phone. "That's all the information I have, doctor. . . . I'm sorry." She fidgeted with some reports on her desk: "Those two post-ops, doctor. . . ."

He looked at her a moment: "You are new here, I believe," he said.

"Yes . . . I am, doctor."

He held out his hand: "The reports, please." She placed them quickly in his hand. With a practised eye he ran through them. Deliberately he handed them back to her: "Nothing critical—I'll tend to the emergency case first."

His step, as he walked towards the elevator, was deliberately unhurried: a lesson for her in the primary attitude required in those who care for the sick. Medicine was a science; emotion, worry, fears had no part in it. Fears were bubbles that burst when you knew what to do—and the doctor knew what to do. He was trained for that, carefully and well. (Hadn't the fidgety woman learned that yet?) There was nothing comparable, educationally, to the wisdom and discipline resulting from his long hours in hospital work.

A hospital was the best university in the world. Everything happened in it: from birth to death; it probed secrets; it faced facts, coldly, efficiently, realistically. And the doctors showed the stamp of their training: they were cold, efficient, realistic —they had to be. In the doctor's hands lay life or death. . . .

He turned the corridor and met an orderly trundling a cart with an oxygen tank. The man stopped and rested on the handles of his cart: "Those two patients on the second floor— I've fixed them up." He patted the dark green cylinder with the condescending superiority of some great surgeon handling a tried and true instrument: "They were in a pretty bad way till I got there."

"Can't do much without air, Roy," he admitted dryly.

"You can say that again," assented Roy with a solemn nod of his head.

"How's the oxygen supply in the emergency room?"

"A little low, I guess, doc. Didn't get a chance to check it yet."

"Better do so after you deliver that one. I've got a patient in the emergency room now."

"Right-ho, doctor. Breath for the breathless, that's me. I'm on my way." Busily he picked up the handles of the cart, and Dr. Powers went on past him down the corridor.

A woman was standing in front of the emergency room, a stylishly gowned woman. With a flurry of skirts and outflung hands she started running towards him: "Dr. Powers!" she cried, "Doctor!"

His smile was polite, his voice unhurried: "What is it brings you here, Mrs. Weatherby . . . at this hour of the night?" Some deep emotion seemed to have robbed the woman momentarily of speech; she flung out her hand in a dramatic gesture towards the emergency room. The smile disappeared from Gray's face: "Your mother? Again? . . . Another attack?"

She shook her head frantically: "No, no . . . not mother," she gasped. "Elaine—she went down in a heap—I tried to get you—"

The strong confident face above her suddenly whitened; his eyes seemed to dilate—and then she was swept roughly aside.

It *was* Elaine . . . slack, formless . . . her dress crumpled, her eyes closed—like one dead!

Blurrily a sound pierced his shocked mind . . . a voice speaking . . . to him. . . . He turned blindly toward it, trying to attend. . . . "It's not an ordinary faint, doctor. . . . I tried all the usual things—"

He saw her then: a nurse, standing at his side—the numbing haze swept from his mind: "Get Roy! Down the corridor —oxygen!" He spun back toward the table.

She had begun to tell him that there was a small amount of oxygen in the cylinder; but she suddenly went dumb, stricken silent by the terribleness of his hoarsely whispered cry: "Elaine! Elaine, dear—" He was bent over, holding the woman's face in his hands, his whole body a tensed, tortured pleading— Sudden comprehension sent the nurse scurrying from the room; but he did not hear her go . . . his cry had brought no response, no movement, nothing. Her flesh was cold beneath his hands; the crimson of the slightly parted lips

78

like a wound in the white of her face; and the heart-beat was a thin, far-off whisper.

He ran across the room to the oxygen tank. The covering would not come free, and he fought the simple fastenings, his fingers all thumbs. What was the matter with him? What was he doing anyhow? Roy would take care of this, Roy and the nurse. . . . Where were they? When would the fools get back? The doddering, slow-footed fools!

He jerked open a cabinet, snatched up a syringe—his fingers felt stiff, swollen, as he injected the stimulant into her lifeless arm. . . .

He straightened up. The hand, holding the empty syringe, was trembling, and he rested the heel of it against the table. . . . His eyes, fearfully impatient, clung to her, waiting for the change that did not come. Her lips did not move . . . her eyes did not open— A tinkling sound suddenly broke the room's breathless stillness. Unbelievingly, he stared at his empty right hand; then, like an automaton, he went down on his knees, and began to pick up the bits of the broken syringe.

Abruptly he became aware of what he was doing and stopped. His head lifted; he could not see the cross fixed high on the wall: he saw only the cabinets, all about him, cabinets filled with things to save life; and their cold glass fronts mocked his despairing gaze. They held nothing that would save her—

He surged to his feet, flinging away the shattered syringe that had failed him. . . . Frenziedly, he seized her hands and began to chafe them, calling out her name . . . again and again . . . beseechingly . . . vainly. . . . She was gone

. . . gone into the black emptiness that was death . . . but the extremity of his anguished love would not admit the fact. His arms pulled her to him, and he covered her face with kisses, begging her to listen to him, to open her eyes, to speak . . . she must not die, she could not leave him . . . he needed her . . . she was his life. . . .

Against his cheek, something moved: a long-drawn, shuddering sigh sounded in his ears . . . and her lips trembled into life. . . .

In an agony of hope, scarce daring to breathe, he stared at her, waiting. . . . The lids of her eyes fluttered, then opened . . . and, for a moment, bewilderment clouded their dark brown depths . . . then, at sight of him, the bewilderment fled, and she smiled. . . .

He hid his face on her shoulder: "Don't move, darling," he whispered urgently, "don't move."

Her voice was a weak thread of confused wonderment, asking, wanting to know— "No, dear, no," he assured. "You're all right . . . you're all right now. . . ." She lay perfectly still, his reassurance all that she needed. . . . And when, after a little space of time, her lips parted and she whispered an endearment, he could not restrain his arms from convulsing about her: "Don't ever leave me, dear . . . don't—"

"O Gray, you are all that I have . . . all that I care for!"

It was a cry of sheer terror; and it cut through his own fear like a knife. He lifted his head:

"I'm here, darling . . . see: I'm here. . . ." He forced assurance into his voice. "There's nothing to be afraid of . . .

nothing. I'll take care of everything." His hands cupped her face, forcing her to look at him, to see only him. . . .

Tremblingly, her hand stole upwards, touching lightly his hair, nestling in back of his head. His strong, confident face was close to hers, each feature, so well-loved and familiar—but there was a mistiness now about those gray-blue eyes—and it drove into her heart, as into an old wound, the memory of when first she had met him: for then, too, his eyes had been wet with tears; and she had wiped them away; and they had gone on laughingly through the bright days of the summer, planning so many things . . . bright things . . . wonderful things, which somehow had never been realized, because, somewhere, in the passage of the years, the brightness of their first love had been shadowed over. . . .

A wistfulness came into her eyes as she remembered, and the memories were suddenly near again and real—living things that murmured from her lips in words that sounded strange in this room of barren walls and loveless steel:

"The quiet waters . . . the little pool, our little pool, where first I found you. . . ."

He looked deeply into her eyes, and understood . . . and remembered . . . "Oh, my dear, my dear!" he exclaimed burying his face against her. "I have been so blind . . . so stupid. . . ."

She held him then, her eyes closed, everything forgiven and forgotten, all fears dismissed, in the all-sufficing warmth and security of their original love.

When the door swung open and Roy trundled in his cart,

Gray straightened up and faced about. The nurse was hurrying fearfully forward, words of apology ready, but his hand, upraised in an authoritative gesture, stopped her. Gray turned to Roy: "Over there," he ordered the attendant, "set it down over there. . . . We won't need it now."

Chapter 9

ELAINE came awake slowly. The room had been darkened, but daylight was bright against the closed blinds. A glance at her watch showed it was late afternoon. The effects of the sedative had not fully worn off, and she felt dull and listless. Slowly she took in the strange room and its almost cold simplicity. There was a chair by the side of the bed—Dr. Arnet had sat there, last night after Gray had gone, asking her questions, many questions, about herself, questions that reached back to the first days of her meeting with Gray. . . .

Hazily her mind drifted over last night's startling events. She could remember clearly enough the constricting pain that had felled her, gasping, to the floor. The memory of it still clung to the back of her mind, but silently and subdued, its terror overshadowed by Gray's love and contrition. She had forgotten nothing of what he had said: she went over his words again, lingeringly, with the delight of a child fingering its regained treasures. And she decided that what had meant the most to her was his impassioned plea for her never to leave him. It told her so clearly how much he loved and needed her—and suddenly she was all impatience to be away from this room, to be with him again, alone together, in the warmth of their own home. . . .

It was such a gracious little home, on a gentle hill, a little world of comfort and charm. Idly, she tried to call up pictures of it: the rooms, the garden, the view from the living-room's spacious window—but the pictures would not come. Annoyingly, they seemed to elude her. . . .

She shifted the pillows so she could sit upright. Almost with resentment, she surveyed the room, as though it were the cause for her inability to daydream lovingly about what had always been a source of pleasure for her. A chatter of treble voices came to her through the closed blinds: "Oh, take one, Tess, just one—go ahead, I dare you." "Sister said not to—" "The red one—the rose." They must be student nurses, she thought, at recreation. The hospital garden must be outside her window. The carefree voices and the light laughter recalled that she, too, had once been as light-hearted. . . . For a long time her love had been perfect, free of shadow. The change, when it came, had been a rude shock, because it had been so sudden. But now, for the first time, she realized it had not been sudden. It had been very gradual—only the manifestation of it had been sudden. And it had been this hospital, Gray's coming here, that had brought it about. . . .

His conduct had hurt her so abominably these past months. The complete absorption in his work she could understand: but his secretiveness, his shutting her away from his plans and thoughts—that had cut deeply. And all his extravagant gifts had failed to heal the wound. For what did it avail to have everything, when what you most wanted you did not have? What attraction could there be in a lovely home *if you were unhappy in it—*

The thought jolted her: it was so startlingly new. But it was the truth: she had not been happy in her beautiful home —how could she have been? Having everything, you have nothing (and happiness least of all) if you do not have love.

There was a telephone at the side of her bed; and the desire to speak to him was suddenly strong within her. But he had to be on duty again tonight: he would be taking his needed rest now. She had always held a faint pity in her heart for those women whose love was such a thin emotional thing that it required endless, repetitious declarations from their husbands of love and devotion. She hoped she was not falling into that abhorred class. Her heart told her with complete certainty all that she wanted to know: their love was completely restored.

With a contented little sigh she nestled back against the pillows, the memory of Gray's stumbling admission of guilt and sorrow a hidden well of contentment within her. She tried to savor again all the joy of that moment. But the piercing sweetness that had gone through her then did not return now. Instead, she was aware of a faint fear stealing over her, the same fear which had overwhelmed her when Gray's frightened voice made clear to her how close she had been to death. She had seen only one person die, and the terror of that moment was nothing like this—when it was yourself that was faced with death—

She had come upright in the bed, free of the pillows, her hands clutching tightly at the bedspread, a fine trembling shaking her body. Dr. Arnet had not told her what her illness was, how much danger— Her hand fluttered out towards the call bell; but when her fingers touched it they dropped away —the signal unsent. She forced herself to lie back on the pillows: she was not like others alone and helpless; she had a sure source of help. . . .

The place Gray now held in her affection, that unique position of love which absorbs and yet fulfils, had been shared by only one other person in her life—her mother. How gentle she had been: her days so filled with work, and yet weaving prayer into her work, as familiarly and easily, as though there were angels standing at her elbow. For all of childhood's poignant little troubles, she had comfort; and for all its problems, answers—ready ones and sweet ones. That little mother had been her world, until she had met Gray. . . .

He was staying with his uncle and aunt who owned the adjoining farm. She had heard of him, but had never caught a glimpse of him till the day that he, totally unaware, invaded the privacy of her own little haven of refuge.

There was a deep pool of water between her father's farm and that of the Powers family. It was a clay pit that had been abandoned when water flooded the workings. Bushes grew thickly all about it, and clusters of young willow trees drooped about its edge. It had rained that morning, but the sun had come through the clouds and beat strongly on the moist ground, filling the air with an oppressive sultriness. . . .

She slipped away to the pool, undressed and entered the water. No one ever came this way, except some stray cattle. The water was silken cool. Contentedly, she sat there, up to her chin, bubbling breath from her lips, and watching the ripples undulate slowly across the pool and die on the opposite rim.

A sound in the bushes on the opposite side brought her head upright. Motionless, she listened: it was not the blundering movement of cattle, but the steady step of a man. Breathlessly, she scurried beneath some overhanging willows.

A solitary figure came into view, a boy, with a cloth-wrapped bundle in his hand. He stood there, staring vacantly at the water. . . . Abruptly, he dropped the bundle and sat down.

For a moment she thought he was intending to take a swim, and she opened her mouth to call out a protest: but before she could utter it he had flung himself forward . . . flat on the ground . . . his face in his hands; and the sound of his sobbing came clearly across the water. . . .

She slipped out of the water and scrambled into her clothes. Hurriedly she made her way around the pool. She had never heard anyone cry as heartbrokenly as this, and she acted instinctively. Edging up to him quietly, she knelt at his side; her hand crept forward and rested lightly on the touseled head: "Please . . . don't cry," she pleaded softly, "don't cry. . . ."

His body stiffened, and a sob seemed to strangle in his throat. He did not lift his head: "Go away," he finally said, "go away. . . ."

She drew away her hand, repulsed by his gruffness, and sat back on her heels, looking at him.

He lifted his head to dart a quick look at her: "Why don't you go away and leave me alone?"

"I . . . I thought you were hurt, or sick."

"I'm not . . . I'm all right." He sat up.

"But you were crying."

"Who was crying?"

"You. . . ." She touched lightly his tear-stained cheeks, and showed him the wetness on her fingers: "See?"

A deep red dyed his neck and face: "That's sweat," he maintained. She did not gainsay him. He stared at her a minute: "You're losing your dress," he observed.

It was her turn to blush. "The buttons in the back—" she explained plaintively, her lithe young body twisting into grotesque contortions as she struggled to reach the unreachable. She looked up at him. "I can't get the top ones."

"Turn around," he ordered. Obediently she turned, and he began fumbling the buttons into place.

Suddenly her hands flew to her throat: "My medal! I've lost my medal—"

"It's back here," he said, and handed it to her over her shoulder, sliding it along the string to which it was attached.

She thanked him, explaining it had been her mother's medal when she was a little girl, and that she never, never wanted to lose it. She smoothed out her clothes and turned to face him: "It is a pretty dress, isn't it?" She had worn it only once before; and she turned slowly about for him to admire.

He stared at her a moment, not rudely, but a trifle abashed, as though not knowing what to do or say. With disconcerting abruptness, he stooped and picked up his bundle.

"Are—are you going away?" she asked hesitantly.

"What makes you think that?" he demanded suspiciously.

She pointed significantly at the bundle. He hitched it up under his arm and turned away.

"You *are* going away?"

"Yes; as far as I can get—from them."

The short angry gesture of his head indicated the Powers farm.

"Your uncle and aunt will be—"

He spun about: "They're not my uncle and aunt," he denied heatedly. "They only call themselves that. They're just relatives, distant relatives. Dad never even spoke of them to me . . . not even once."

"But they will feel bad if you run away?"

He did not care how they felt: "All they do is scold and preach: I must save; I must learn the value of money; I must

not be like my father—they think he was no good; because he
didn't charge people! I hate them . . . I hate them . . .
they killed my father!"

In his fury he flung down his bundle, and the cloth flew
apart strewing its contents about the ground. . . . She
stared at him, and the frightened look in her eyes brought
about a quick change of mood: "You don't have to look at
me like that," he said shamefacedly. "I'm not mad at *you*.
. . . What are you scared about?"

"What you said," she explained slowly. "It isn't true. Your
uncle and aunt were here all the time. They never went away
except to bring you here. They couldn't have killed your
father."

"It was people like them that did," he retorted. She looked
at him blankly. "That's why I hate them," he shouted angrily,
"and they know it . . . and they hate me. . . ." Abruptly his
anger was spent; his shoulders slumped and he thrust his
hands dejectedly into his pockets: "Everyone hates me."

"I don't hate you," she said protestingly.

He looked at her with puzzled eyes: "How can you—you
don't even know me."

"But you just told me all about yourself," she objected.

"I didn't either," he denied, "not everything." He thought
over matters a moment. "What's your name?"

"Elaine."

"Mine's Gray Powers." He stooped swiftly and picked up a
little leather folder that had spilled from the bundle. "This
is my father."

She took the picture and looked at it intently: "He smiles

—so easy and loving like," she observed, "just like my mother does." She looked up at him, comparing. "You don't look like him, Gray . . . maybe . . . if you smiled?"

He shuffled his feet uncomfortably.

"I—I can't," he said. "Not now."

He reached out for the picture, but she drew it to herself. "Aren't you going to tell me about him?"

He stared: it seemed strange, after the way his uncle and aunt had spoken, that anyone should be interested in his father.

"I . . . I can't. . . ." But she was waiting, her face eager, her lips slightly parted. And so, in a few stumbling sentences, he tried to tell her about the goodness and the greatness that lay behind his father's easy smile. And then (because it was so terrifyingly fresh in his memory) he began to describe the terrible change that had come about: the growing thinness in his father's face; the tiredness; the pain that he passed off with some chuckling remark; the slowness in his step as he went about caring for the sick, in the squalid, sprawling town. For weeks and months he had done this, smiling away his own pain, until he could no longer rise from bed. . . .

There had been nurses then, who stayed, day and night, with his father. They were not paid. His father had no money. They did it for nothing—because they liked him. They were good to his father; but he did not know that at first. He was jealous because he could have no part in the things they did for the one he loved. He used to watch them, alert for he knew not what, but determined that, if ever he should detect them doing anything that would discomfort his father, he

91

would do terrible things to them. But they never gave him cause to carry out any of his wild resolves. . . .

The night nurse was soft-voiced. He could not remember his own mother; but she must have been like this nurse. She seemed to understand what it was that he wanted and needed. She allowed him to sit, hour long, by his father's bedside. And, when the dumb choking anguish within him seemed to be no longer bearable, she would reach out and take his hand and pat it comfortingly, coax him away from the room, and fix a warm drink for him. . . .

By slow degrees, he came to accept and then to love that white-garbed woman. Her trim cap and uniform impressed itself upon his mind as a symbol of something clean and good and strong, something that could face calmly and bravely the dark evil that was pain.

There were days when a moaning sound could be heard coming from his father's room: a low, steady, persistent moaning, that gradually mounted in intensity. Filled with terror, he would run to the door of the room—but the nurse would not let him in.

And then one day, that whimpering, helpless sound drove him mad. Frantically, he forced himself past the nurse and into the room. . . .

Distended gray eyes stared at him—enormous eyes, that did not recognize him—empty eyes, blind with agony. Frenziedly his hands clawed the nurse: "Make it stop: please . . . please . . . please!"

"I can't, child, I can't," she said helplessly. "The doctor will not allow it . . . it would kill him."

He had crumpled up then on a chair in a storm of heart-sick, helpless sobbing. . . .

There was no memory of what followed: only an awareness of a burningly deep and enduring promise that he had made to himself: whatever it was that had done this terrible thing to his father, he hated . . . and he would hate it always. . . .

They took his father away to the hospital, and he had gone to see him, for the last time, the day before he died.

The bewilderment, the fear, the helplessness of those last moments together showed again in Gray's distended eyes as he recalled the details: the man, who lay on the bed, he did not know. It was not his father; it was some stranger, a ghost, with pain-wearied eyes—but suddenly the eyes lighted up, recognizing him . . . and then it *was* his father. The flesh-less fingers opened slowly, in the comradely way of old for exacting a promise. And he had gone down on his knees at the side of the bed, thrusting his hand into his father's, squeezing it hard: "Oh, dad . . . what is it you want? . . . what is it? . . . what must I do?"

The words of reply were only a dry ghost of sound: "The little places . . . son . . . the little people, the needy ones—"

In an agony of waiting he knelt there, tears spilling from his eyes, as he watched his father fighting for breath that would not come, and for words that he would never speak.

The nurse finally led him away. And that night his father died. . . .

They brought the body home; and there was a dim memory

of people coming and going . . . many people . . . surging all about him and past him . . . women crying quietly . . . men muttering prayers . . . grimy laborers whispering, in stricken voices . . . outside the room where the coffin stood . . . surrounded with flowers and flaring candles. . . .

It had rained early in the morning, the day his father was buried; and a pall of leaden gray clouds covered the sky. The somber evergreen trees, lining the main road in the cemetery, dripped sluggishly with moisture; and the dense throngs of mourners, filling the spaces between the trees, made the road seem a long dark corridor. Down it he stiffly walked, in his new dark suit, with the black band about his upper arm.

A shaft of sunlight suddenly slanted downward through a rift in the clouds, and, in its pitiless light, there was only himself and that open grave at the far end of the walk. . . .

He wanted to break and run: but he could not. The silent people and the somber trees were solid walls hemming him in; and he could only go forward, toward that small square of darkness in the earth, that waiting emptiness that would swallow him up, and it would be ended . . . everything would be ended. . . . Deep inside of him, something seemed to twist and break with sickening suddenness—and he was all pain and blinding tears and hopeless longing for a love that was eternally ended. . . .

The clods of earth that had fallen on his father's coffin were like the blows of a hammer nailing shut a door, closing the room where his father had dwelt, ending the life that he had known. . . . He was taken away to his uncle's farm and its unforgettable desolation of cold mornings, early rising, and unending chores.

His uncle and aunt had no children, but they were aware of the responsibility a child entailed. From now on he was their responsibility: his upbringing their special care. Dutifully they attended church each Sunday and compelled him to go with them. They were not concerned so much with allaying his grief as with saving him from his father's foolhardy attitude toward life. They spoke to each other, in his presence, pointing out the sinfulness of a man who cared so little about economy as to keep no books about the moneys due him. . . . "Charity was all right, but it had its limits. . . . Give people a finger, and they soon had your whole arm." And the real tragedy of Dr. Powers' life was that, knowing this, he yet had allowed people to take advantage of him.

When Gray had angrily shouted a defense of his father, he had been summarily disciplined. Alone in the cold darkness of his meager room, he would lie in bed, trying to submerge the hurt of the moment by the happiness of the past. And the picture which most frequently arose was of his father seated by the fireside of a winter evening, his light gray eyes sparkling, as he told him stories of their adventurous forebears. There was one who had been an explorer (a grim sort of scientist he was); and there was the one his father had called the "swashbuckler" (there seemed no end to his madcap exploits); and then there was his grandfather, the captain of a ship, part of an expedition into the Antarctic. All of them had had their faults; they had been headstrong and passionate; but to his father they were great men, crusaders, going where others feared to tread. . . .

Eventually he slept. There were never any dreams. Just an interlude of nothingness between one day and another. And each day became more unbearable in the company of this uncle and aunt who thought about nothing but money and food and work.

In desperation he had decided to run away. But somehow, when seated here alone, looking at the quiet pool, the hopelessness of what he intended to do had risen up in him and broken loose. . . .

Gray looked up at Elaine, shamefacedly (because of the tears she had seen), wondering if she understood.

Eyes, soft with sympathy, met his. Impulsively, she reached out and took his hand, and smiled at him. And, in some magic way, all his unhappiness was gone, dismissed, by the enchantment of her smile. . . .

She knelt down and gathered up the things that had spilled from his bundle. And, when she was finished, he took the ends of the cloth and tied them together: but he tied them lightly, for he was not traveling far. He had run away, and he had not run very far: because he had found what he was seeking. . . .

Together they walked into the beauty of April, and she showed him all her heart's treasures. She taught him to see the goodness there is in the untouched things: the contentment of the cloud-dappled fields, the delight of the downfalling rain, the joyousness of the abounding sun, the otherworld aloofness of the dove-song mourning from the thickets that fringed their quiet pool.

And he became for her the god, who walked always protectingly at her side: at times broodingly dark, at times exuberant with memories of his father and with high-flying dreams of greatness.

Their moments together were always stolen moments. He never entered her home, and he never wanted her to be seen by his stern-visaged guardians. She knew that she was his secret delight, that he wanted to share her with no one. She was content with that; and, all the more readily, shared with him her dearest possessions: her quaint beliefs in heavenly things, her custom of mingling little prayers with earthly needs and joys. . . .

But, as the months and years of early youth slipped by, she saw a gradual change come over him: his father still remained for him a great man; but he had been an impractical one. Medical skill was a valuable thing, just as any other skill was. To give it away freely was sentimental foolishness. His father could have been a rich man if he had just had some business sense. . . .

Elaine was shocked the first time she heard him speak this way. Gray's admiration for his father had been the trait that first had drawn her to him: it was so deep and true. She had loved him for it; and she had to protest what seemed like betrayal. A doctor was not just a merchant. People had loved his father because he had thought of them—and not of money. And they had shown their gratitude. She reminded Gray of the imposing headstone they had set up . . . the street named after him . . . the editorials extolling his father's greatness. (She had mounted them in a scrapbook for Gray.)

But all of that meant nothing now to Gray when weighed alongside of the fact that his father *had not been a success.*

The way he stressed the words almost precipitated a quarrel. She accused him of believing everything his uncle said; and she made no secret of her displeasure. But that did not change him. "I was displeased, too," he reminded her, "even furious when I first heard that idea expressed. I thought my uncle cruel, unjust." But he had not been that: he was merely being honest. The more you thought it over, the plainer it became. His father had acted unwisely: he had given everything and gotten nothing. In life you had to be hard and demanding and sure. Everybody else was. And if you did not fight your way to the top you were soon lost in the swamp of failures underfoot. . . .

In his dying moments his father had finally realized that; and had wanted to keep him from making a similar mistake. With his final breath he had tried to tell him that . . . "the little places . . . the little people, the needy ones . . . *they have brought me to this end!*"

The nurse entered Elaine's room with a professionally cheerful greeting. Crossing to the window she drew up the blind. As she came over to the bed she began the usual polite inquisition—had she slept? was she feeling better?—but the abstracted expression on Elaine's face halted her. She turned and began to shake down the thermometer. Torpidly, Elaine submitted to her ministrations, answered some routine questions, and with something of relief, saw her finally depart.

The light outside seemed less glaring. It was evening, and from the garden below came the liquid cooing of mourning doves, bringing nostalgic memories and a faint sadness. It was very clear to her, at that moment, that what had gone out of her life, had gone out long ago: from the moment he knew the meaning of his father's words, Gray had changed— and all his ensuing actions and behavior derived from that change.

In the blindness of her self-conceit, she had always imagined that she had been the inspiration for Gray's becoming a doctor. She had been ill once (with some sort of distressing fever), and when she had told Gray how the doctor had allayed her suffering, Gray was openly envious. It was then that he had confided to her his intention to be a doctor: not just an ordinary doctor—a great one, like his father—but a successful one, too.

With shining eyes he had then shared with her a hitherto closely held secret: he had a legacy, a portfolio of notes (page on page of them) left him by his father. They were a study on arthritis, with a projected line of research for establishing a cure.

His wild ideas and extravagant plans about the possibilities of this legacy brought a tender little smile to her lips. She knew him so well: these moments of exuberance were natural to him. They came and went; this, too, would pass. But how wrong she had been! This had not been just another of his daydreams: this was something rooted so deeply in him that,

compelled by it, he had determined to become a doctor—
and not because of her. . . .

Dr. Arnet was a pragmatist. Among the students at medical school, his following was a flatteringly large and attentive
one. His recognized medical skill was matched by several of
the other professors, but not the pungent commentaries on
life with which he interlarded his lectures. Gray was in the
forefront of his admirers. Nothing could have been more
natural and inevitable: for many of Arnet's acid-tipped remarks gave exact expression (and what was more important
—direction) to ideas which up till now had been rather nebu-
lous in Gray's mind.

As Gray had once shared with Elaine all the past but lost
joys of his childhood, so now he confided to her the present
wonderment and delight of this new-found influence. He
gave her the names of books Arnet had recommended, and
she faithfully read them, trying to keep up with his advanc-
ing development. . . .

By means of his letters she walked with him the wards of
a New York hospital, during his months of internship.
Through his intense eyes, she saw and registered a thousand
unforgettable sights: the twitching lips; the sucking breaths
that were like a prayer for the air of life; the malignant
growths, the ulcerated wounds. As a child he had seen pain
destroy his father. Here, in the crowded wards and assembly-
line surgeries of a great hospital, he became aware of the
universality of pain's attack upon man. . . .

The hate that he had had for pain became an obsession,

a crusade. He fought pain as something personal. His devotion to duty, his growing skill and painstaking tenacity became a byword among all his associates. And when he went on to postgraduate studies and then research, she uttered no word of complaint. In her heart there was a firm resolve not to interrupt the course he had set for himself.

Sorrow has high walls, and there is no gate nor gap in them: only love has the strength and skill to scale them. The sudden death of Elaine's mother brought Gray swiftly to her side. How gently yet surely had he pierced the vast isolation that seemed to have descended upon her! It was then that her affection for him had been most deeply felt. With the mute trust and sureness of the flower seeking the sun she had turned to him: and he had not failed her. His gentleness and love had filled up the aching emptiness in her heart. . . .

He was impressive looking now: broad-shouldered, tall, and his years of training had set their seal upon him. He moved with deliberateness, and his assured, measured way of speaking was the trait of a man she did not know. He had changed. But when he looked at her his eyes still held the same frank affection as of old—and she knew nothing had changed.

One day they had gone to their old haunt by the side of the pool. As they sat there beside the tranquil water, she sensed that a mood of great restlessness had come over him; and drawing his hand into her lap, she had looked up at him, wordlessly inviting his confidence.

He had started slowly, but then the words gathered momentum as the dammed up flood of the years was released; and all his hopes and aspirations poured forth. He told her how he dreamed of medical science as an army drawn up against a dark enemy, an enemy with a million masks. Each unit of that enemy had to be tracked down, the source of its power bared, and then destroyed. It was a foe of a million masks, but the patience and intelligence of medical science were stripping aside those masks . . . putting names to these nameless terrors . . . controlling their ravages . . . and in some cases destroying them. . . . A faraway look came into his eyes as he envisaged this fascinating world of opportunity; there were no limits to the rewards it held out for the successful: fame, fortune. . . .

A faint fear came up in her heart, and she heard his voice only as a vague sound, running on and on endlessly. Her fingers slid away from his, and stole upwards, touching the necklace about her neck. She lifted it, looked at it, studying the intricate, gold setting. It was his gift to her.

Aware of her lack of attention, Gray stopped speaking. The water of the pool was quiet, unruffled. There was no sound: only the gentle cooing of the doves in the thickets, like a mocking echo to all his passionate speech. He waited, but Elaine did not lift her eyes to his.

"Why all the silence?" he asked

"I—I was just waiting."

"For what?"

Her little smile was apologetic: she had just been wondering if he had forgotten—or perhaps it just did not mean anything to him any more?

"Maybe it doesn't—whatever it is," he replied with a shrug. "You drop certain things as you advance. If you are going places you must travel light. I thought you understood."

She protested that she did; but "Aren't some things too much a part of your own real self to ever be left behind?"

He looked at her and smiled placatingly: "My dear, I included you . . . very distinctly . . . in everything I said."

"But not your father."

He stared: "My father? . . . What on earth has he to do with this?"

The gentle reproof in her glance surprised him; it was not her way to be critical of him or his behavior: "You are putting overmuch importance on something that is not important, my dear," he advised. "I know that at the present moment, because of your bereavement, a memory may seem something highly sacred. . . . You must not forget that I, too, went through a similar experience. But, as time moves along, a memory is just a memory—I haven't forgotten my father. But to be dragging a dead man into everything I say or plan would be plain morbid—and you wouldn't want me morbid, would you?"

She smiled a trifle defensively: "No, of course not. It's just that—well, since the time that you alluded less and less to your father, you seem to have been speaking more and more of money."

"Please—Elaine!" he protested quickly. "I'm not interested in money. Really I am not. That is a matter that will take care of itself. All that I want is to know that you are on my side—with me all the way."

"You know the answer to that," she chided, "without my telling you."

"Then why were you looking so unhappy a moment ago? If you had lost your dearest possession you couldn't have looked more—" Her tell-tale blush brought sudden insight: "Why, it's that old medal you used to wear!" he accused. "You are still missing it—"

Haltingly, she defended herself: there had been so many happy little events, so many memories connected with it.

"But I thought you had grown up? Your letters—the things you wrote. I thought you were free of all that pietistic nonsense about rosaries, medals, and the rest of it." It was more than disappointment that showed openly in his face. Her failure to see eye to eye with him on this small matter had hurt him.

"It is your necklace I am wearing, Gray," she said with quiet significance, "and not my 'old' medal."

His gaze darted up to hers, and the love and loyalty he saw in the soft dark eyes quickened a sudden tenderness in him. He moved swiftly, his hands cupping her cheeks, as he pressed his lips against her mouth: "I'm jealous," he admitted softly, "terribly jealous—even of your sentimental memories."

"You need never be, dear," she murmured reprovingly. All the things he had written her; the books which at his direction she had read—the impression received from them was very vivid and real to her. Childhood had its own make-believe joys; but for the adult only reality sufficed. She was adult now, and free. "And I've never been so happy, Gray. . . ."

With gentle fingers he tilted her chin upwards, his eyes looking deeply into hers: "Stay that way, dear—always."

Elaine had a strange little faith in the fulfilment of wishes expressed for others. If they were sincerely unselfish they would see fulfilment. She had a deep inner sureness about this. The source of this belief she never questioned, nor whether it was fact or fancy. She simply took it for granted that unselfishness had in it some strange hidden power for fulfilment.

Certainly, the happiness, which Gray's unselfish love had desired for her, had permeated all her married life. It had deepened as their intimacy grew. More and more she had come to view life, and all its aspects, through his eyes. But now, for the first time, it struck her as strange that despite this growing identity of views there should have appeared, these past months, a widening chasm in their affections. Could there have lain hidden, through all these years of seeming happiness, some destroying selfishness in their love? The old endearments were still spoken, but they had lost their meaning. Something intangible was at work; and vainly she had tried to come to grips with it. All the ingenious devices of her love were unavailing to start the spark in the cold ashes of Gray's affections. In desperation she had proposed they have a child. . . .

She had not known what his reaction would be. At the

outset of their marriage she had agreed to his firmly expressed conviction that children must wait until his financial position was assured. Long since, the point had been reached and passed when the advent of children would have worked a financial hardship on them; and gradually she realized that Gray's lack of interest in a family was due to his absorption in personal ambitions. For that reason, she made her suggestion, a trifle timorously. But her fears were groundless: he readily agreed to it; his financial status warranted the expense. That he should have based his consent on that factor alone was further indication to her how far his love had cooled.

As the months of her pregnancy advanced his attitude did not change; the outward form of love was there, the inner spirit was flown— And yet, what her impending motherhood had failed to do her sudden illness had achieved!

The thought was bitter-sweet: she had had to be on the very verge of death before his love for her revived! What had she said? "The verge of death. . . ." The dark circle of her thoughts had come back to the fearsome truth that had been its starting-point: for truth it was that last night, in the emergency room, she had been very close to death— it had been the narrowest of margins.

Her previously vague fear was now open panic. Convulsively her eyes clamped shut, trying to shut out terror as though it were a visible thing. But it stayed; no thought of Gray or his words and love could shake it, and through her terror drove the shattering certainty that her real happiness—

her freedom from fear—had been the time *before she had met Gray!*

It broke across her tortured mind like a burning flash of light: in its pitiless brilliance all her compliant love seemed a horrible treachery. "O God," she whispered brokenly, fearfully, "what have I done? . . . to myself? . . . and to him?" Tremblingly, her fingers groped upwards: but they did not find what they sought. There was only his necklace there now. Helplessly, her hands fell to her sides; and the tears came: tears of rending remorse and abject pleading. . . .

A shoe scuffed heavily on the parquet flooring, and, lifting her head, Elaine saw through the blur of tears, a white-haired priest standing at the side of the screen, which masked the open door: "I'm Father Chriswell, the chaplain," he said; and then, seeing the apprehension that flickered into her eyes: "No," he reassured her quickly, "your doctor did not send me—there is nothing to fear. I was just making my rounds," he explained, "and your door was open."

Her fear went swiftly from her. He stood there so simply, like the answer to a prayer. A gratefulness came into her eyes: "Won't you come in, Father."

He gave a grave little nod of acknowledgment and came towards her. "May I be seated, Mrs. Powers?"

She smiled at his formality. "My friends call me Elaine," she said.

Chapter 10

"BEEN waiting long, Hil?"
From the depths of the easy chair Dr. Arnet's startled gaze darted upwards. Gray, dressed in a dark blue lounging robe, stood looking down at him. "I had left word with the housekeeper," he added, a trace of reproof in his voice, "to call me when you arrived. There was no need to sit here waiting."

Arnet moved into a more upright position. He had forbidden the housekeeper to disturb Gray. Doctors needed their rest, and besides he had not minded the wait. In fact, a little peace and quiet had been very agreeable. He gave a little sigh: "It has been a hectic day." One hand gestured lazily towards the picture window. "The view you have is restful. A man could spend a lifetime here, and be content."

"A lifetime?" Gray elevated an eyebrow. "That is too big an order for me." He placed a chair in front of Arnet and sat down in it, blocking out the view of the distant mountains, and the distracting beauty of their wine-red coloring. "Well— what is the verdict?"

The unconscious air of superiority beneath the words and action sent a quick little flash of anger through Arnet. He did not relish being treated as an old shoe, remembered only when the pinch came. "Cardiac," he blurted out; and then added, "as you probably surmised—"

He broke off, ashamed of the sarcasm the moment it was spoken. Gray must still have affection for Elaine: and, in any event, it was no way for an attending physician to give a report. But Gray's attitude, since his success in obtaining the reasearch, had become maddeningly irritating. It had reduced their friendship to such a low ebb that he would have let him face this present trouble alone, if Elaine were not concerned. She meant a great deal to him; and at one time she had also to Gray. Watching him now he began to wonder. Gray had pulled a packet of cigarettes from his pocket, and his hand was steady as he selected one.

"Are you sure?" he asked.

His wife a cardiac, and the extent to which it affected him was this bald question! Two spots of color appeared in Arnet's cheeks: "Of course I'm sure! The sedimentation rate is elevated, and the E.K.G. is indicative of myocarditis—" Gray was calmly putting flame to his cigarette; and suddenly nothing mattered except to pierce that callous self-sufficiency: "And that isn't all—" Deliberately he let the ominous silence draw out.

Gray drew heavily on the cigarette and exhaled.

"No?" he prompted. "What else?"

"Rheumatic fever . . . definitely."

The expression on Gray's face did not alter, but the cigarette slipped from his fingers to the floor. For a moment he stared at it lying there, smoldering . . . then he leaned forward, picked it up, and dropped it into the ash tray. Slowly he came to his feet and walked over to the window. . . .

Against the backdrop of the distant mountains, the tall, broad-shouldered figure seemed small and insignificant. . . . His air of importance had vanished: he was just a solitary, lost, little figure of a man, bewildered, stricken, by the sound of two spoken words. . . . Rheumatic fever.

Gray stood there, trying desperately to assimilate the shocking truth Arnet had discovered. . . . There had been the illness she had had as a child. To her it had been just "some fever. . . ." It had probably been the first attack—He spoke without turning: "How bad is it?" he asked.

"Bad enough: another attack may occur any time." Arnet shrugged. There was no need to detail the rest: the advanced state of Elaine's pregnancy and that she was a primipara. Gray was a doctor, an intelligent doctor—he knew what had to be done.

Gray waited as though expecting his friend to say something more, to offer a suggestion. But Arnet's unrelenting silence told him that the decision was being left squarely up to him.

He turned and walked over to a small desk. There was a letter-opener lying on the polished surface; he picked it up and tapped the blade against his open palm. "A Caesarean," he decided, "at once."

Arnet shook his head:

"There are still some days to go before the hospital will allow that. . . ."

The outer edges of Gray's eyebrows flared violently upwards; and Arnet, mistaking it for amazed incredulity, halted. Evidently Gray's claim (that he knew exactly how and why this hospital functioned) had been an exaggeration. "There is no hope," he explained, "for the child to survive—if the operation is performed now. There is—if you wait the additional time. That is why the hospital will not countenance—"

"I said . . . a Caesarean . . . *at once.*"

The cold hostility in the way Gray spaced the words seemed to leave Arnet unimpressed: "I understood you," he said coolly.

"Then why retail this hospital's moth-eaten ethics to me?"

Arnet was placidly stripping the cellophane wrapping from a cigar. "Because you plan to stay in this hospital. . . ." From under the arched eyebrows a sudden frosty glance darted upwards. . . . "The research . . . remember?" He bit off the end of the cigar cleanly. "If you have the operation on Elaine now, and the hospital learns about it—" His hand made a slashing gesture towards his throat. "If you wait the

required number of days, she can have the operation . . .
right here . . . with the hospital's full approval."

Gray stared, as the import of the words reached him. Arnet
thought that the all-important consideration for him was to
keep the research: that he would sacrifice anything and
anyone for it. Amazed indignation filled his voice: "Just
what sort of man do you think I am?" he protested.

Arnet's eyes glinted. Gray could blame himself for any
wrong impressions—if they were wrong. He reminded him
of their recent talk. The distinct impression created by Gray's
words had been that nothing was going to keep him from getting the research job. "Logically, I concluded that nothing
was going to keep you from *holding on* to it—"

"You actually believe that I'd expose Elaine to suffering
. . . and death . . . in order to hold on to the research
job?"

The thin lips twisted. "Wouldn't you?"

"No!" It was a defiant shout. "And even if I would, *I
don't have to*! Haven't you thought of that? We can operate
on Elaine without the hospital knowing anything about it."

Arnet nodded ready assent: "But," he pointed out, "there
would always be the danger that they might find out about
it."

"I will risk that." There was a hard, sure recklessness about
the way he said that. "If the hospital finds out they will rescind my contract. So what? I'd rather lose a hundred research jobs than Elaine." He studied Arnet intently. "Satisfied?" he demanded. Arnet did not reply but the lipless mouth
gave signs of relenting. Slowly Gray crossed the room, sat

down and faced his friend: "I will need you with me on this, Hil," he said.

Thoughtfully, Arnet rotated the cigar back and forth in his fingers. Gray's declaration of need had mollified him, and what he had said sounded sincere, but he had to be sure. "There is a new school of thought," he replied judiciously, "which advocates allowing the pregnancy to go to term, claiming that due to the new techniques, the risk can be greatly minimized—"

"Stop acting the professor, Hil," broke in Gray, irritably. "I know all about that. The risk is still there—they admit that—and *there must be no risk for Elaine!*"

The passionate vehemence of his words brought a surprised look into Arnet's eyes. For a moment, he studied his friend as though discovering some unknown quality in him, then he glanced down at the tip of his cigar: "If I were in your place"—he broke off momentarily, then shrugged—"I could only do what you intend to do. Elaine's life must be the primary consideration."

All the tension seemed to go out of Gray, and an extraordinary warmth of friendliness for Arnet's loyalty surged through him: "I rather felt you would agree." The stiff formality, almost smugness, of his words surprised him. It had not been what he wanted to say, and he wondered why he could not express the gratitude he really felt at the moment. "There is just one other item: how much have you told Elaine?"

"Nothing . . . as yet." For a moment he seemed to hesitate, and then: "I thought it better for her to learn of her

113

condition from you. She should be more amenable to the operation . . . if she sees that it is what you want."

Gray fixed his friend with a quizzical glance. "You haven't any doubts, have you? . . . About Elaine?"

Arnet grunted: "It's an operation. And no one wants to hear that word even mentioned."

Smilingly, Gray put that aside as an evasion. And when he accused him, point-blank, of thinking Elaine might be difficult for other reasons, Arnet reddened slightly. "But you're all wrong," maintained Gray. "Elaine will go along with us all the way. . . ."

Abruptly Arnet stood up: "Inform her then about her condition and what has to be done. . . . As soon as she agrees to the operation I can order her to be removed from the hospital; and we can arrange for the surgery to be done elsewhere."

"Why wait? . . . Make the arrangements right now. Elaine will agree."

"Am I in charge," snapped Arnet, "or you?"

The anger blazing in those frosty blue eyes startled him. What on earth was coming over Arnet? He was becoming as touchy as a boil, and it was destroying that free give-and-take that had formerly marked their friendship. But his present need of Arnet's assistance made it imprudent to start probing into the reasons for his hypersensitive behavior. He could not risk antagonizing him. . . . In a conciliatory tone of voice, Gray explained he had had no intention of dictating. It was just that Elaine meant so much to him—and right now every hour could be important. He capitulated:

everything would be done as Arnet wished. "I'll see Elaine this evening," he promised, "and get her consent for you."

Seemingly mollified, Dr. Arnet got to his feet. At the door he turned, and his face was devoid of expression, as though his gust of anger had completely passed. "I suppose you realize, Gray," he remarked casually, "that you are going to be in this section of the country . . . for quite a long time?" Gray's expression showed no such realization: on the contrary, his stay here was to be a very brief one . . . merely a stepping-stone to other and bigger— "Because of Elaine," explained Arnet softly. "This climate has proven helpful for rheumatic fever cases. . . ."

A sudden quiet seemed to come over Gray; and his eyes narrowed thoughtfully. If Elaine must stay here, he, too, would remain. And that fact held some unpleasant implications. If the hospital were to rescind his contract as head of the research, the stigma would make it impossible to start up a private practice here. . . . It could be an awkward state of affairs: condemned to reside in a locality where all the doors of opportunity were closed to him. . . . He glanced sharply at Arnet's unrevealing face. It was impossible to tell whether malice or a discreet, persistent friendliness had prompted his disturbing observation. But if Arnet imagined for a single instant that after winning the gamble for the research, he was now going to resign it and start up a stodgy private practice— "I'll call you," he decided with brisk finality, "as soon as I have Elaine's express consent."

Chapter 11

IT WAS late when Gray came to Clayton's room. Some unforeseen delays, while making his rounds, had occasioned his tardiness. Sandra was on duty and informed him that Clayton was asleep. She caught the slight annoyance that flashed across his countenance. "There was a hypo prescribed," she reminded him, "for 8:30. . . ."

It had slipped his mind. He should have visited Clayton first instead of last. At his request Sandra gave a report on the patient's condition. He listened to the swift, sure phrases, noting her strictly professional attitude. "She is back in her proper place now," he thought to himself, "and it will not be difficult to keep her there." With a curt nod of acknowledgment, he took his leave. . . .

He had phoned Elaine earlier telling her that he would visit her; but there was no light showing as he approached her room. He was careful to make no noise as he entered.

Moonlight silvered the bed where she lay sleeping, the abundant tresses of her dark hair framing the white oval of her face in loveliness. She seemed but a child, defenseless, innocent—and a warm feeling surged up in his heart, a soaring sense of personal sureness.

Unmoving he stood there, savoring this sensation of sweeping power that the mere sight of Elaine could evoke. He had never sought the reason for it. He had never wanted to. It was satisfaction enough to have it; because along with it there was a dim awareness that it could only be the result of a love that was unique. And, for a moment, he was strangely stirred by the mystery of this love which had come out of nowhere and linked him and her, irrevocably, together. . . .

A nurse's step pattered down the corridor; the phone at the main desk rang once, faintly, followed by immediate silence; and then there was the small quiet sound of a door closing. . . . All the world was asleep, but the hospital never rested. It was an eternal vigilance, a voiceless strength —awesome in its utter singleness of purpose. . . .

Gently, his fingers touched Elaine's pulse: it beat rhythmically, calmly, unaware of the dangers that threatened— and love came up in him in a great tide of trembling tenderness.

A dimensionless greatness seemed to fill him; and, for the space of a heart beat, he was one with the silent strength, the ponderous power of the hospital. For he knew that there was in him this same strange quality of singleness. It was this driving thrust of concentrated power that set the hero apart from the herd; and the lack of it was the reason why so many climbed a lot of small hills, but never scaled a mountain. . . .

Elaine's delicately fringed eyelids fluttered and then opened. For a moment, the dark eyes, staring at him, were the eyes of a stranger—and then recognition lit a warm little glow in their depths. She murmured his name, and he leaned forward, lightly brushing her lips with a kiss. "Do you care to talk for a while or—"

She turned towards him, readily acquiescent, her hand seeking and finding his . . . The white oval of her face held a soft dreaminess, a pensiveness—or was it contentment? Somehow he had not expected her to be like this, and he feared that what he had to tell her might shatter this mood of great peace.

But her fingers tightened, with slow gentleness, about his, urging him . . . and so, in a few words, he gave her Arnet's diagnosis. Perhaps, he thought, she was prepared for this. The recent heart attack must have given her a premonition. But she would not be aware of the after-effects. He spoke more slowly and calmly, explaining about the resultant cardiac condition which could make childbirth dangerous, even fatal. "So we will have to tend to the pregnancy at once," he summed up. "There will be no danger to you, dear . . . not if we have the operation immediately."

The hand that he held did not tense nor make any effort to withdraw, and he wondered if the disappointment was so sudden and sharp that it had shocked her into this complete immobility. Anxiously he scanned her features: "There is nothing to be worried about, dear," he reassured her.

She was no longer looking at him; her attention seemed to have centered on her other hand, which lay close against her side, a tightly held fist, hidden from his eyes. Slowly her gaze came around and met his. "I want to have the child," she said simply.

A look of puzzlement spread over his features, as though he had not heard aright—but her steady gaze assured him that he had.

He forced an indulgent smile. "Of course, dear, of course. I can understand that. But there is no help for it: it is you or the child—and so you will just have to be realistic."

"I intend to be," she said gently, and then with no tremor of emotion in her voice: "An operation now would kill the child. . . . It would have no chance . . . and the child must have its chance."

He drew back. "This is no time for heroics, Elaine—I am deadly serious."

"So am I, dear, as never before in my life." Her hand lifted, and the fingers opened, disclosing something dark huddled in her palm.

He leaned forward slightly, and as he recognized the object his whole body seemed to stiffen: "Who gave you that?" he demanded in a harsh voice.

"The chaplain," she replied. "I asked for them."

He stared as though hypnotized. It was an inanimate thing cupped there in her palm, a rosary, beads strung on a chain, black beads, as black as treachery, as black as death. . . .

The one and only rival to his love he had eliminated (so she had led him to believe) long ago, before they were married, on that day when she had agreed that there would be nothing else in her heart or mind except him. . . . And now, with a single gesture, with a few words— He held back his anger, remembering her illness. There must be no disturbing scene. Bitterly he realized that he had been living for years in a fool's paradise. "I thought you loved me," he said, and he could not keep the hurt out of his voice.

"I do, Gray, oh, I do!"

"You can prove that," he suggested, "very simply and easily, my dear."

She looked at him pleadingly; but there was no wavering in his eyes, no yielding in his will. Sadly, yet firmly, she shook her head in refusal.

And it was his gaze that dropped in defeat. . . . Her outstretched hand still held the beads . . . and, suddenly, he knew that those beads *were* death: for they were the end of everything between him and Elaine. . . .

It was past midnight when he drew up the car before his house. He paused a moment in front of the door, fumbling for the key in his pocket. Far off, from the center of the town, a locomotive clanged its bell, and the sound of it filled the night's emptiness. A train was coming in; a train was leaving; the thin night air of the desert carried the clamor of distant, rumbling, rushing wheels. Abruptly, the whistle of the train sounded: a hoarse, gigantic cry from the iron throat of the machine, like a soul-searing shriek of pain.

Blindly, Gray thrust the key into the lock and stumbled into the darkened house.

The bewilderment and anger that had come down on him made sleep impossible. Agitatedly he roamed up and down the living-room. His cheeks burned with the remembrance of the words he had spoken here: the arrogant assurance he had given Arnet that Elaine saw eye to eye with him on everything!

What a blind fool he had been! Imagining that he knew a woman's mind, because he loved her! Imagining that she loved him, because she had smiled assent and seemingly agreed! How many times . . . in this very room . . . she had woven her web of flattering insincerity about him! All the memories of their intimate moments were suddenly become a torturing bitterness; and the shadows in the far corners of the room seemed to mock him for having, like a lovesick fool, planned and built the edifice of his life, with her as its center and inspiration. Did he imagine she was different from the rest of women? their unpredictableness? their whimsies? It was of their nature to inspire—and to destroy. He had given himself and the carefully built castle of his ambitions into her hands. It was hers. Why should he be outraged if she now chose, with a petulant finger, to topple everything into ruins?

Like an engulfing wave, anger rode over him: anger at Elaine's unforgivable duplicity, at her treacherous yielding to another love than his. But there was even greater anger at himself; because—in spite of what she had done—he still loved her! She was his. He wanted her. He would not let her martyr herself!

He started towards the telephone, and stopped. . . . He could not call Arnet; Elaine's decision had made a complete fool of him in Arnet's eyes. There was only one way to redeem himself: he knew what it was; he knew what he must do. Why did he keep turning away from it? Why did he keep searching for other possibilities?

There was no other possibility.

He had to be ruthless to be kind: he had to remove her from the hospital . . . without her consent!

He stopped his restless pacing and asked himself, wonderingly, why he had been hesitating. This solution was so simple and sure. . . . The small subterfuge that it entailed was one that every doctor had to use on occasion with a patient—the sick so rarely knew what was for their own good. . . .

The whole atmosphere of the room seemed suddenly changed. The shadows no longer mocked: they were a friendly dark, holding memories of Elaine . . . of confidences here given . . . of thoughts exchanged. She loved me once, he assured himself, and her original surrender was real, sincere. The radical and sudden change that had come over her was due to the hospital. Her illness and consequent fear had made her an easy prey to its insidious theorizings—helped by her own childhood sentimentalities.

The first flush of his anger had abated, and he could see

clearly how the hospital had worked upon Elaine's sense of guilt to compel her to their way of thinking. "The child must have its chance . . ." Their specious reasoning had induced a faint sense of guilt even in him! Elaine was no traitor—she was a victim. Plainly, it was his place not to condemn, but to save. . . . And suddenly he was sure that he could. Once he had her back here with him, free of outside interference, he knew that his love would prevail. . . .

He was standing at the window, and as his resolution crystallized he became aware of the scene outstretched before him. To his right, lay the town: a cluster of lights, a little world of gaiety and life. Far off in the west crouched the unbroken dark of the desert, a dimensionless beast, inching up, stealthily, on the unsuspecting lights of the town. . . . And, between the dark and its prey, there stood only one rampart: the hospital. . . . It stood there alone, a fortress of unearthly white, four-square to the dark, formidable, fearless, forever, as though into it the dark could not come. . . .

He spun about, crossed the room, and swept his fingers, forcefully, across the light switch. There was a sharp click, and the room was plunged into complete darkness. He stood there a moment, alone in the dark, and there was no sound except his breathing; it had the shallow, uneven tempo of a man tensed for attack. Then he turned on his heel, and his footsteps made a hard, determined sound in the emptiness of the house, as he mounted the stairs to his bedroom. . . .

Chapter 12

THE shrill ring of the telephone at his bedside awoke him. He sat up, trembling; the terror of his dream still startlingly real. The phone continued to ring insistently; and his hand, mechanically, reached out and found the receiver. . . . "Good morning, doctor," said a bright voice, "it is past eight o'clock. . . ." Puzzled, Gray stared at the dark all about him. It was morning, and yet it was so strangely dark, and the dark seemed part of his dream's unreality, its bottomless void, and that sense of falling. . . . The voice on the phone stopped, waiting his answer. He mumbled an assurance that he was not ill. (The heavy drapes across the closed Venetian blinds—that was the reason for the room being so unearthly dark.) His mind cleared: "Tell them to carry on with the work they were doing yesterday— Yes, Sister, they know. . . . I'll be there in half an hour."

He got up, swept aside the drapes and drew the blinds. The flood of sunlight was dazzlingly real. He flung wide the window and drew in deep breaths of the dry, crisp morning air. A cactus wren whistled shrilly, and he stood there letting the freshness and reality of the new day wash away the unreality of the night's feverish dreams. . . . Faintly, across the brightness of the morning came a sound: the far distant wail of the ambulance's siren, rising and falling, surging forward and receding, thrusting its way into his consciousness and enveloping him again in the dread formlessness and fear of his dream.

He was striving to move forward, to answer the desperate need of some low-moaning cry, which rose and fell with the dread monotony of a person rocking back and forth in pain— but a dead weight held him: an invisible weight that was gathered about his knees with the compelling softness of a child's clinging body. . . .

And out of the sound of the moaning pain there emerged a face. In the dimensionless dark it flowered forth: the face of Elaine; and the breathless beauty of it was marred by the haunting sadness in her eyes. The invisible weight at his feet held him as he surged forward. He stumbled. Then viciously, fiercely, he struck downward at it. He struck only once; and, though his hand felt no resisting flesh or body, he was free.

He lunged forward then towards Elaine and brought up short as though he had struck a wall. Horror-struck, he saw

125

the loved countenance contort, the lips writhe, the eyes turn stricken . . . and it seemed to be not only in anguish but in loathing . . . because she was going backward, away from him, merging again into that horror of dark out of which she had come.

Something seemed to burst in his brain. He shrieked aloud her name . . . and the tortured sound of that single despairing cry was still in his ears as he plunged headlong after her, and found himself falling into an unending blackness . . . an unanswering silence. . . .

He stood there at the window of his room, his eyes haunted and fearful. . . . And, for some unaccountable reason, his mind went back to that time when he had slept like the dead, without dreams, because there were no longer hopes or fears—the time after his father's death. . . .

The purpose of the conference, Dr. Bromwell explained, is to settle several major points of policy, so that henceforth the research could function independently. . . . "Publicity," he proposed, "should be integrated with the progress and scope of the foundation's efforts." With a dull hopelessness, Gray longed for an interruption to the long-winded discussion; he wanted to talk to Arnet. His phone call at lunchtime had been without results. Arnet was out on a call. A personal snub could not have irritated Gray more deeply. There was in him a feverish impatience to put into action his decision of the previous night. And this conference was going to take up the whole afternoon. . . . "The danger of mistakes," announced Dr. Bromwell pontifically, "will be minimized in this undertaking, just as in any other scientific enterprise, by a dispassionate appraisal of our objectives, and a scientific detachment in our decisions." The words had a strange effect upon Gray. His unwonted impatience, he suddenly realized, could be merely a blind. Decisive action was important, of course, but that was not the basic motive for this unwonted urgency. I am acting, he told himself, like a schoolboy about to raid someone's apple orchard—I'm in a guilty sweat to get it over with! What an odd notion that was! A feeling of guilt could only come from wrongdoing: and what he proposed to do— "Am I becoming infected with the hospital's crazy ideas of what is right and wrong?" he asked himself in angry amazement. . . . There had been that dream last night—that idiotic dream! That was it, of course. He had allowed himself to be influenced by something as unsubstantial as the meaningless images of a dream.

As he walked away from the conference room nurses went busily past him, carrying trays for the evening meal. He decided to stop and see Clayton. So much time had been lost because of the conference that he knew he was going to be late for his evening rounds, and if he were going to see Clayton it had better be now, before he had his sedation. Besides, the present moment was not the best for talking to Arnet: he would be taking his evening meal, and to be called away from the table always made him ill-tempered. . . . Almost angrily he brushed these considerations aside and started for Clayton's room. He knew the real reason for wanting to see Clayton—why cover it up? He just wanted to disprove that fatuous feeling of guilt. . . . It stood to reason, he argued, a guilty haste would not be diverted from its purpose in order to tend to someone else's problem, especially if that problem is totally unrelated to its own.

No one responded to his light tap on the door, so, thinking Clayton might be asleep, he turned the knob quietly. A little girl was seated at the side of the bed, her blond head buried in the sick man's lap. . . . Clayton's eyes lifted and stared at him blindly; and the naked suffering in that gaze had the impact of a blow.

With a quickly murmured word of apology, he stepped back out of the room. It was a reflex, as swift and sure as the upflung arm warding off a blow. For, at sight of the sorrowing child and father, something had stirred into sudden life within him: something piercing sharp yet compassionately tender—something he wanted no part of, at any time, and least of all, right now.

Sandra had come up beside him and was studying, with faint apprehension, the forbidding lines of his countenance. He was not aware of her until she spoke.

"His daughter is with him," she explained. "He wanted to be alone with her."

His attention focused on her, but the expression on his face did not change.

"You should have remained outside the door . . . immediately available, if needed."

She murmured an excuse: she had not known it was necessary to be that vigilant. "Should I restrict the visits of the child?"

"Why do you ask that?"

128

His bluntness brought a surge of color into her cheeks. "A child should not have to look on pain—not that kind of pain."

A strange, twisted expression flashed across his face. "Then why did you allow her in?"

She hesitated a moment, but it was not for lack of a reply. She had kept the patient's need primarily in mind in making her decision: and had expected Gray to readily understand and approve. But now she did not know. . . . "He has so little time left," she finally ventured. "I—I thought whatever happiness he can get—"

"Happiness?" His hand shot forward, the index finger rigidly pointing at Clayton's door. "Go in there: look at those two."

The sudden sharp command, the open indignation in his voice, for a moment, confused and slightly frightened her. . . . But his relentless look showed her that it was not just a rhetorical gesture he was making to impress her. So she turned and carefully edged open the door. . . . After a moment, she as carefully drew the door shut and slowly turned to face him. He gave her no chance to speak: there was no need to speak. Now she knew how emotionally upset her patient was from this visit, the harm it had worked by sapping the little vitality remaining. "Every minute of life is precious . . . doubly so, when a man's hours are numbered— From now on, that child may not see her father— except when I judge fit. Do you understand?"

She turned her eyes aside, not wanting him to see the fury of protest they held. What was important about life if life held no happiness? If to have a few minutes of happiness

129

you had to pay for it by losing some drab hours of existence, the price was small, the exchange profitable. There could be joy in the midst of suffering—*if love was there*. Did he not know that? At this very moment there was joy in her heart because she was near him . . . even though he was hurting her so abominably. Time, life were not precious; they were nothing . . . unless they held love. But, of course, he did know that—far better than she. But love, for him, was on another plane; and, because it was, it made every moment of any man's life not only inexpressibly precious but sacred. . . . Her voice was abject as she promised that she would follow out his orders to the letter. "If it is so important to you . . . I mean, life, every moment of human life . . . . if it is so sacred to you, I want it to be for me, too."

Her face was lifted to his, and so she saw the almost stunned look that came into his eyes. Fearfully, she asked herself what she had said. She had agreed with him, hadn't she? Why, then, did he look at her that way? . . . His eyes were empty and cold, with anger—or was it something else?

"There is very little breathing space left in Clayton's lungs. . . ." He spoke the words stiffly, his eyes focused on some indeterminate point above her. "See to it that he does no smoking: he might choke up on us. . . ." He seemed to wrench his gaze back to her: "Make a note of that—in writing."

In a small voice she murmured docile assent to his orders, but her eyes were intent on his, silently begging for more than just this return to the stiff, hateful footing of nurse and doctor . . . but he spun about and strode away.

Chapter 13

S HE stood there, staring at his retreating back, her whole
body quivering with the hurt that he had inflicted. . . .
His swift, striding step told her that he had completely lost
patience with her—he, who was so patient!

But what did he expect? That in a few short weeks she
could be as he was? Was there to be no allowance made for
her weakness, no sympathy for her efforts, not one small
smile for her love to feed on?

Bitter, burning tears of futility choked up in her throat.
Her hand lifted to her cheek, to brush away the evidence of
her weakness. Stupidly she stared at her hand as it came

131

away. It was dry. There was not even to be the solace of tears.

She stood there, sick and desperate, asking herself what she must do to put herself right with him again. There had been but brief snatches of sleep during her period while off duty, and they had been disrupted with wild-eyed dreams and imaginings. And she knew this was due to his attitude towards her the previous day. She had found an explanation for that, but this hopelessly confused her. She was unable to see what it was that had been wrong in her conduct, yet she told herself there must have been somthing wrong or he would not have been so peremptory, and cold, and strange. . . .

"My dear, what on earth is the matter with you?" The head nurse was at her side, solicitously holding her arm. "You look positively ill."

There was nothing but honest concern in the face bent towards her, but Sandra could scarce repress the sharp retort that rose to her lips. What right had this busybody to go prying into her secret affairs? With difficulty Sandra managed to murmur a reply: she was just feeling a bit upset . . . nerves. . . .

"Why didn't you inform me?"

"I was hoping it would pass, Miss Osbourne . . . it isn't anything really serious."

The gimlet eyes, behind the horn-rimmed spectacles, kept boring into Sandra's countenance, as though seeking, waiting for a fuller explanation. And then, when it was evident that

Sandra did not intend to amplify: "Take a turn in the garden," she ordered. "I'll substitute here for you." She glanced at her watch. "Report back in thirty minutes."

It was a moonless night; but the radiance streaming from the hospital windows made shiny ribbons of the garden's cemented walks. Sandra walked aimlessly past shadowy trees and dark shrubbery. She came to a sudden halt: she must have been walking more rapidly than she had known. This was the far end of the garden, and the chapel's façade blocked her path—a flat, dim whiteness, with the deep dark of its arched portal seeming to beckon invitingly. For a moment she was possessed by the absurd desire to plunge headlong into it, to bury all her fears and desires and confusion in the dark silence of the place of worship. But it was just a passing impulse. She turned her back on the building. She wanted no walls about her at this moment. Her own confusion and futility hemmed her in tightly enough. . . . She walked away from the path, toward a clump of shrubbery. Here she was free of the sight of buildings: there was only the sky above and the sweep of lawn beneath.

The fresh dark enfolded her, bringing momentarily a sense of peace; and with it there came a remembrance of the night when all this quiet darkness had been strung with lights, and these carpet-like lawns had been crowded with chairs and people. It was at the far end that the platform had stood and the Commencement speaker, who had extolled the greatness and glory of the nursing profession. . . . Her fingers lifted to touch the nurse's pin affixed to her uniform. Meditatively she fingered it, recalling the things Gray had told her that night. . . . The wonder of that had never left her. She alone of all the graduates had been without friends to share the joy of this great event; and he had sought her out, and by sharing her joy had doubled it. . . .

How desperately she had tried to live up to all he had counseled—and this was the result! Her confusion came back upon her in a devastating wave; and with it a sense of anger that he should expect so much of her. And she knew that this anger was justified: he had acted unreasonably. She had a right to be angered and to give free rein to her feelings. But she could not. She had opened the door of her heart, and a new presence had entered in, possessing, ruling the whole house of her thought and affection with an autocratic power.

She began to walk back toward the hospital, and she was not aware of it. Her thought was centered on one fact: there had been a misunderstanding between them . . . it must be cleared up immediately. There was only one way to do that: swallow her pride and hurt feelings; go to him, and ask him, humbly, to explain what she had said that was wrong, what it was he had expected her to say. . . .

As she drew near Gray's room she saw that his door stood invitingly open, and yet her step imperceptibly slowed. . . . It was so important that she say the right words this time—and she did not know what the right words were. She could see into part of the study, and no one was there. Hesitantly, she took a step forward to see better. The room was empty. She stood there, held by a disappointment so sharp and sudden she wanted to cry. And suddenly his voice came to her, loudly, irritably, from the adjoining room.

"Yes, that is what I said: Elaine is determined to risk her life in order to have the child. . . . What do I intend to do? Why, stop it, of course. . . . Yes, yes, I know . . . but this is not really Elaine's decision—the chaplain talked her into it—and the only recourse left us is to get her out of the hospital *without her knowing it.* . . . Once she is at home I can convince her to have the Caesarean. . . ."

Stupefied, Sandra stood rooted to the spot, her mind dazedly fumbling about with what she had heard, trying to find an import in the words other than the one they held. . . . But there was no other: what she had heard could mean only one thing—

". . . Glad you agree, Hil. . . . Elaine's life must be our first consideration." His voice held satisfaction now, assurance. "Well, we could do it this way: call the head nurse and prescribe a narcotic for Elaine; an hour later notify the desk that you intended to discharge her in the morning, but you have just learned that I would like to take her home this evening, when I go off duty. . . . That ought to allay any suspicions. . . . Right. . . . No, I don't think you need have any fear on that score: she *will* listen to me—I guarantee that."

Her eyes wide with shock, Sandra backed away from the open doorway. . . . It was not true! It was not Gray saying that! It was someone else speaking—and she would not listen to any more of it. She twisted about and ran down the corridor. . . .

135

DARK ENEMY

Gray put down the receiver and lit a cigarette. Thoughtfully, he squinted at the spiraling smoke. Tomorrow was his day off; he would be free of the routine work of a resident, but the research—he would have to arrange to handle that in the afternoon. The morning must be entirely free so he could be with Elaine, undisturbed— The phone rang suddenly, startling him: but it was only the desk: a maternity case had just been brought in; he was needed in the delivery room. "I am on my way," he announced briskly.

Chapter 14

IN THE dim light of the room the face of Clayton was a blurred yellowish mask against the white of the pillow. The hypo had failed to put him to sleep, and instead he had become unusually talkative. He had babbled about everything: but always, with the persistence of a refrain, he had come back to his petition for "a little smoke—just one cigarette—what harm could it do?" Sandra's patience had worn thin refusing him, repeating Dr. Powers' orders and trying to explain the reason for the injunction. It was with a sigh of relief that she saw him finally lapse into silence.

There was only the rasping sound of the sick man's breathing. She stood silently at the bedside. From the open window

there came the eerie expiring sound of the ambulance siren
as it approached the hospital entrance. . . . Her mind slid
away to her own problem: the snatch of conversation, so
fortuitously overheard, which had upended her world; she
was faced with a decision on which the lives of others literally
depended— The voice of the sick man startled her: "You
ought to talk to the chaplain," he said. She leaned forward.
Had the man been reading her mind? But his eyes were
empty of recognition. "Amazin'," he confided to the world
at large, "the things he believes. . . . He tol' me—know
what he tol' me?"

The slurred syllables were evidence that the hypo was
beginning to take effect. Quietly, Sandra drew away from
the bed and crossed the room to the open window. In back
of her Clayton's voice had the remote meaninglessness of a
brook babbling steadily in the empty night. She stood there,
one hand at the side of the window, gazing out into the night-
shrouded desert, blind to the glory of the star-swept skies,
seeing only one thing: in her hands lay the fate of the one
she loved. . . .

And she could do nothing. She had to stand here and wait
until the drug took full effect upon her patient. Duty held
her here, bound her, even though a higher duty had laid its
demand upon her. For what she intended to do was just that:
a higher duty. That had come to her so clearly during her
moments in the chapel. . . .

As from a great height she could look back now upon her
conduct these past weeks and wonder about the impatience
that had consumed her because of her slowness to change.

She had not realized that change is a growth: and growth
goes on slowly and unseen. She *had* changed: remarkably
so. How else explain the unerring instinct which had sent
her, at the moment of crisis, to the chapel? . . . Huddled
there in the dark, with only a single red lamp flaring fitfully
near the altar, she had found the courage to face the pitiless
facts: it *had* been Gray speaking those cold-blooded words,
coolly planning a crime. . . . And all the beautiful ideals he
had spoken of to her—what were they? Some monstrous deceit he had practised on her? It could not be: no man was
that vile, that low—Gray least of all.

Yet, trapped by events, he was about to do a shocking
wrong. And she loved him—as never before she loved him,
with the deep possessiveness that comes from complete
understanding. For, with absolute sureness, she saw through
this mystery of evil into which he had fallen . . . because she herself had once fallen victim to it. Had not love
for her mother once driven her, tricked her, into demanding
the easy and immediate solution? Had not fear of losing the
one she loved distorted what was coldly evil into compas-
sionate mercy? He had saved her then, and she would save
him now.

The little red flame of the lamp floated brightly in the
dark above the altar: a flame of faith, and hope, and love. . . .
Steadfastly it burned, unknown to most of the world, through
all the hours of the night and the day. It never died: for faith
and love were unquenchable . . . and hope eternal. . . .

The far-off heights were suddenly very near. It required
but a single step for her to mount to where Elaine stood:

a renunciation equal to Elaine's. She could save Gray, but—
she could never tell him that she had. If Elaine lived, she
had exposed her to death; if Elaine died, she was the cause
of her death. On either count Gray could only hate her; and
so, her part in saving him must never be disclosed. Her generosity held nothing for herself—everything for him. She
risked discovery and loss of any hope for winning his love. . . .

It was a frightening prospect. It could mean the death of
her most deeply held desires; and yet there was in her a
strange thrilling eagerness to embrace it. She lifted her head,
and the martyr-red glow of the sanctuary lamp seemed to
flicker approvingly as she came to her feet and hastened
from the chapel. . . .

There was a telephone booth in the lobby, and she could
call Elaine from there. It was a dial phone and would not
disclose the source of the call.

So intent was she, so keyed up to the sacrifice, that she
thoughtlessly hurried into the hospital and headed straight
for the lobby. Too late she saw Miss Osbourne coming towards her. . . .

One swift look of appraisal seemed to satisfy the head
nurse. "There is a hypo prescribed for your patient now,"
she reminded Sandra. "Will you tend to that immediately?
I am needed at the desk."

There was nothing else she could do but go back on
duty. . . .

The vital minutes were slipping by, filling her with a
mounting tempest of impatience and exasperation. It was not
because of the sick man. In her heart there was no word of

blame for him: only a vast compassion. It was the delay, caused by her own stupid lack of discretion, that was driving her frantic. Somehow this enforced period of waiting was dulling the fine edge of her high purpose. In the chapel she had felt the exaltation of sacrifice sweep over her like a wave, lifting her to a dizzyingly glorious height. . . . But now, other considerations kept insidiously intruding: if she told Elaine about Gray's plan, Elaine would refuse to leave the hospital . . . and so the child would have its chance at life— *but Elaine might die.* And with Elaine out of the way— A fierce, dark joy suddenly shot through her. She shivered slightly in its pleasurableness, the entrancing possibilities—

A car roared up the driveway, and its glaring headlights swept across the open window. She took a step backward, blinking violently like one suddenly awakened. Slowly she turned. The room was as it had been, depressingly dim; but the patient was strangely still. . . . She went up to the bedside. For a second she stared at him, the closed eyes, the regular rhythm of his breathing. He was asleep at last. . . .

Swiftly she went to the door and peered out. There were some visitors in the corridor, huddled together, talking in low voices, outside the door of some desperately sick friend. They made a compact group that would effectively screen her departure. She slipped out of the room and went swiftly down the hall. . . .

There was a small quiet click as the door closed; and Clayton's eyelids lifted heavily. With ponderous slowness, his head turned, peering carefully about the room. Faint satisfaction showed in his eyes as he saw that he was alone. His hand reached out and opened a drawer in the bedside table. From beneath some handkerchiefs he drew the package of cigarettes. A slow smile crooked his lips. Roy had readily responded to a man's need for a smoke. He lit the cigarette and drew the smoke hungrily into his lungs. A spasm of coughing shook him. When it had passed, he drew back his head and surveyed the cigarette disapprovingly. . . . After a while, he started to bring it up again to his lips. . . . He had it half way to his mouth, and then, as though an infinite weariness had overcome him, his eyes closed, and his hand drooped slowly downwards. The cigarette's tip formed a hot brown spot on the coverlet . . . a faint smudge of acrid smoke arose . . . but Mr. Clayton slept. . . .

Chapter 15

AS GRAY came out of the delivery room a man placed himself in his path. He was dressed in an inexpensive blue suit, shiny with much usage. Mutely he stood there, blocking Gray's path.

Puzzled, Gray darted an inquiring glance at the nurse standing in back of the man. She gave a slight nod of assent, a tolerant smile touching her lips: "The waiting-room was too far away," she explained. "He wanted to be near her."

Concern and expectation seemed momentarily to have deprived the man of speech. Gray's hand closed down on his shoulder with friendly pressure, assuring him that everything was all right: "They are fine—the both of them. . . ."

A gusty exhalation of relief came from the man, and then: "Guess I made a nuisance of myself," he confessed shame-facedly, "but I was worried. . . . Is it a girl?"

"Yes, a girl."

The man's face lighted up: "That's swell. I've got two boys." He fumbled out a cigar and thrust it at Gray: "It's a twenty-five-center," he explained with a touch of importance. "A friend gets them for me wholesale when the blessed event comes around." Gray was sniffing experimentally at the cigar. "They're a real smoke," assured the man, "and if you—" He shot a quick smiling look at him: "You're married, aren't you, doctor?"

"Yes, I'm married."

"Well, if you come to need cigars," he twinkled knowingly, "just let me know . . . I'll get this same brand for you, and at the same rate. . . ."

"Thank you. I'll remember that." Gray turned his back and walked away.

At the elevator landing there was an urn, filled with clean sand. He jammed the cigar deep down into it until it was completely out of sight. Mechanically his fingers dusted some sand into the hollow.

A tiny light at the side of the elevator glowed redly denoting that the conveyance was in use. Gray glanced at his watch. The narcotic should have taken effect by now and he could remove Elaine. All his calls were attended to except Clayton. He would doubtless be asleep (there was a hypo prescribed for 8:30 o'clock) but he would check, just in case, on his way down. He pressed the button to summon the elevator.

The corridor was deserted. The happy father must have scurried down to his wife's room by way of the stairs. . . . The emptiness of the corridor seemed to make it grotesquely longer. Idly, he kept staring down its length . . . and after a while he became aware of the vague sense of unease that was stealing over him. Coupled with it there was a sort of dread expectancy. . . . Irritably, he asked himself what it could be that brought on this strange mood so frequently. What was he waiting for? What did he expect to discover in a corridor? There was nothing here, nothing but a stretch of emptiness: the doors at one end, and he at the other—

There was a click, and the door of the elevator slid open in back of him. He spun about and stepped into the well-lighted cage. . . .

The head nurse was not at the desk; and Gray's heels made brittle, echoing sounds as he went past on his way towards Clayton's room.

Carefully, he edged open the door: the room was in semi-darkness, only a night lamp illuminating one corner of it. Sandra was bent over the patient's bed, her back to him.

He spoke softly, so as not to awaken the patient: "Is the hypo still holding?"

Sandra's head jerked about, her eyes staring at him over her shoulder. She was like some savage creature, crouched in fear, lips writhing soundlessly. . . .

He started forward, but her horrified whisper stopped him in his tracks: "I—I think he's dead."

He plunged into the room and swept her aside. . . . Clayton's face was contorted, cyanotic: "Oxygen!" he snapped, and, ripping off his jacket, flung it toward a chair.

He did not hear the strange whimpering sob as she ran from the room; he was already above the inert figure, his hands applying pressure and releasing it, falling and withdrawing, as though striving to remind the dormant muscles of their vital function, coaxing them to start up again the ebb and flow of breath that was life. . . .

Into the absorption of his task there intruded some persistent, disturbing sensation. . . . He pushed it from him, and doggedly labored on; but it was still there, a vague uneasiness in the back of his mind, a lurking danger. It was strange, and it was familiar, an odor, an acrid odor, as of burned cloth. . . .

His eyes darted about the room. The window was wide open; there was no semblance of smoke—and yet the odor seemed all about him. He looked down at the floor. Protruding from beneath the bed was a crumpled coverlet, a large section of it browned and blackened. . . .

From the corridor there came the noise of hurrying footsteps. With one quick movement he swept up the telltale coverlet, wrapped his jacket about it, and jammed it into the corner of an easy chair. . . .

He had barely time to get back to the bedside when the door was flung open, and an attendant trundled in an oxygen tank. The head nurse and Sandra crowded in after him.

146

Swiftly, silently, tensely they went to work; but all their efforts were unavailing. And, when Dr. Powers finally stepped back and flung out his hands, there was as much anger as defeat in the gesture. "We have lost him," he said.

The head nurse glanced methodically at her wrist-watch and noted the time. A slight frown creased her brow: "I shall need some details . . . additional details . . . for my report," she observed, turning toward Sandra.

Gray intervened: "I'll make out the report: you can get all the necessary details from that."

She murmured her thanks, directed Sandra to prepare the body, then, with a gesture to the attendant, signified that their work was done. The two of them went from the room.

Sandra moved slowly, with a heavy careful mechanical-ness, her eyes averted, fulfilling the task imposed. She brought some things from the bathroom: a basin of water, a wash cloth, a comb. She set them on the table beside the bed; and then, covertly, her gaze went downward, to the place on the floor, where the burned coverlet had lain. Not finding what she sought, her eyes lifted slowly—his face was like flint. She shrank away into the deeper shadows of the room, and stood there, wordless. Relentlessly, he came around the edge of the bed and stood above her, and she could not lift her eyes to meet his. Remorse and horror were like a clogging sickness in her throat.

"I left the room," she admitted in a low voice.

"I know that. . . . *Why?*"

The single sharp syllable seemed to transfix her. She

stood there, scarcely breathing, the thrust of his word deep in her—and suddenly an indefinable change came over her. She drew a deep breath, and her eyes lifted quickly to his. The attitude of a culprit was gone; and in its place there was a sort of pleading hopefulness, an expectancy, almost an assurance—

"Why do you look at me like that?" he demanded.

Her lips parted quickly as though to reply, and then, as abruptly they closed.

"If you have any explanation," he warned grimly, "you had better make it—now." The expression on her face puzzled and disturbed him. "Answer me. Have you an explanation?" Dumbly, she gave a little nod of assent. "What is it then?" he grated. "Tell it to me." The thrust of his words seemed to send her shrinking away again from him.

"I—I can't, I can't," she whispered desperately.

"Were you sick?"

"No."

"Were you seeing someone?" The guilty blush showed he had hit the mark. "Some silly date was more important than a man's life?" he probed pitilessly. Her stricken face was full confession. His hand shot forward, fastened on her nurse's pin, and ripped it off: "You're not worthy to wear this. . . ."

She stood there like stone: "I didn't think—" she began in a small voice.

"You didn't need to think—you knew! The care of your patient comes before anything else. . . ." He flung a hand towards the bed: "I warned you—expressly—about not letting him smoke. . . . You had your orders—"

148

He whirled, as knuckles rapped on the door; but it swung open before he could start towards it. The head nurse stood in the doorway:

"There's a call for you, doctor: third floor, room three—"

"I am not finished here yet," he replied shortly, and turned back toward the bed.

"I'm sorry, doctor," she apologized, "but Sister Martha said it was urgent: room three-one-three."

He started: "Three-one-three! Did you say room three-one-three?"

She glanced at a bit of paper in her hand, and nodded confirmation: "Three-one-three," she said.

Elaine's room! What had happened? What had gone wrong?

"I'll sign the death certificate when I return." He spoke with forced calmness. "Have it ready, please."

Deferentially, the head nurse stepped aside, and as the door was closing she turned to Sandra, remembering her indisposition earlier in the evening: "Are you sure," she asked solicitously, "that you can handle this alone?"

Chapter 16

MOMENTARILY, Gray halted on the threshold. . . . Elaine was sitting upright in bed. There were no oxygen tanks, no worried nurses, no signs of any emergency. . . . Vastly relieved, he stepped into the room, quietly closing the door in back of him. He went up to the bed: "What is it, dear?" he asked.

Her eyes flicked a glance upwards at him, then looked down at her hands folded in her lap.

"Are you all right?" he persisted.

She replied, without looking at him, "Yes, I'm all right, Gray."

He bent forward, studying her countenance: "They said

150

it was urgent. . . . What is it, dear? Why did you call me?"

Her head lifted, and, for a long moment, her eyes looked into his; then her gaze turned away, meaningly toward the bedside table. A hypodermic syringe lay there—and he saw that its contents had not been administered! His gaze jumped back to Elaine, and in her eyes he saw knowledge, reproof, and sadness:

"Gray," she said quietly, "from now on, Dr. Bromwell will take care of me."

He took a step backward, as though she had struck him. For a moment he stood there, his eyes wide with incredulity and affront. . . .

"You've ruined me . . . everything I worked for—" Despair choked his utterance.

In an odd, detached sort of way, she shook her head slowly, denying his passionate accusation: "I am leaving it up to you," she explained, "to see Dr. Bromwell and arrange the change of doctors."

He stared at her, his despair giving way to wonderment. She had remembered him—even while making her drastic decision! As though looking on a stranger, he stared at her. What mysterious element had entered into her love for him, prompting her to safeguard his interests at the very moment she condemned him to the loss of his all-important interest— herself? The faint glimmer of tears in her eyes sent a stab of pity through him, of sudden tenderness; and he wanted to go down on his knees to beg and plead, to allege his love—

"I know, Gray," she said sadly. "It was your love for me: that was your motive. But, no matter how much you love me, the child has a right to life. You know that, dear, you must know it. It is deep in the heart of every living creature. . . ."

He swung away angrily. "Please, not that! . . . Don't preach . . . not at a time like this. . . ."

But his anger could not deter her: "You are a doctor," she insisted gently, "and a doctor is a healer. It is his place to safeguard life . . . not to destroy it."

Violently, he spun back to face her: "What was I supposed to do? Let you kill yourself? Let you go through all the agony of childbirth, with your heart in the condition it is—and do nothing about it? Do you think I love pain? I hate it—in any shape or form—I hate it!"

The sudden burst of passionate denunciation left him trembling and vaguely startled. In the shocked stillness he felt strangely small and horribly embarrassed, as though he had exposed some darkly hidden shamefulness. And somehow the way Elaine looked at him only added to that sensation: her unwavering gaze was more reproving than any words could have been. It infuriated him: this attitude of sanctimonious superiority; this insufferable pity that moved her to speak in the voice of a mother, infinitely patient with a fear-stricken child: "Gray, Gray dear—"

Something seemed to snap in his brain: "Stop it! Stop it!" he cried. "Don't call on me. I can't help you, I can't change you. I can only love you . . . love you like a fool! You think I possessed you. That's a lie. You possessed me. Everything I've done was for you. . . . Everything I hoped, planned, and worked for was for you—and this is the way you repay!" In a bitter burning flood his pent-up emotions swept aside the last vestiges of self-restraint: the injustice of her decision, the inexplicableness, the cruelty of it—why? Why did she do this to him? He had wanted only to keep suffering from her, and now . . . "you inflict it, deliberately, on me—on me—who can't defend myself . . . because I love you!"

Her white, shocked face seemed to dissolve into a blood-red mist. . . . If she attempted a reply he did not hear it; he was aware of nothing, except this horrible, shuddering fury of betrayal and despair that shook every fiber of him like a sickness. . . .

When his mind cleared, he found himself staring at his hands, with a strange intentness and puzzlement . . . for his hands were calmly going about their task, as though no inner turmoil had ever shaken the very center of his being. They were dipping in and out of a basin of water; handling a brush; scrubbing, diligently, up and down the sides of the fingers, meticulously, across the rounded close-cut nails. . . . There was a nurse at his side, and she moved restlessly, shifting her weight from one foot to the other, as though impatient at his deliberateness. Some task of great urgency must lie before him.

He lifted his eyes, and, through the small window in the wall, he looked out into the delivery room. And the woman, who lay on the table, he recognized. But, strangely, she was no longer just his patient, Joyce; she was someone mysteriously identified with his own self by reason of this dark stream of pain that coursed through his heart as well as through hers. . . .

153

The blurriness lifted from his mind, and the broken sequence of events was restored: the nurse, coming hurriedly into the room, after his furious outburst . . . her words, clipped, breathless: Joyce was in labor . . . hemorrhaging; he was needed at once. . . .

He had turned to go, and Elaine had spoken: "You must not go. . . . Gray? . . . Get some one else . . . you are not in a fit condition to—"

Defiantly, her own words had leaped from his lips in reply: "She's in danger. . . . I'm a doctor—'and a doctor's function is to safeguard life.'"

What he had done or said after that, he could not recall. But he was here . . . in the delivery room . . . gowned in white, his hands steady, his mind reaching forward, with an almost hypnotic absorption, to the task that lay ahead, as though it could by that absorption block off the pain that was in his own heart. "No," he said to the anesthetist, "no general. . . . Her chest condition will not tolerate it. . . . It will have to be a spinal—"

Joyce's voice was a thin thread of protest: "I don't want that."

He stared at her, dumbly, for a moment: "You must have something," he finally said. But she shook her head in stubborn refusal. "The pain will get worse," he warned.

"It doesn't matter. . . . I want to hear my baby cry."

"The spinal will not prevent—"

"You'd better hurry, doctor," urged the nurse. "She is hemorrhaging . . . badly. . . ."

His gaze kept going to Joyce's white face all through the

ordeal. The flesh about her eyes puckered tightly with each new onslaught of pain . . . her nostrils seemed to pinch inward and grow thinner . . . the teeth gritted together, locked and set. He had seen many childbirths, but never such uncomplaining courage.

And when, at the end, she lifted pain-dulled eyes to him—eyes that were wondering and pleading—and asked, in a voice that was a whisper, "Why doesn't my baby cry?" it took the last ounce of his own courage to give her a reply:

"I'm sorry, Joyce. There was nothing we could do. The boy is dead."

The drained face convulsed, and from between the tightly closed lids, tears spilled silently down her cheeks. Her bloodless lips opened, and he bent forward to catch her words: "I wanted him . . . dear God, I wanted him!"

Quickly, he averted his gaze, unable to look upon the tragic hopelessness in that face. His hands moved deftly, surely, doing their work independently of his mind and the fury of protest within it.

Why had this been allowed? Why pile agony on top of the pain she already had? It was inhuman, unjust, cruel. To see courage like hers crumbled into dust was an outrage. She had asked nothing for herself, nothing but what any wife had a right to expect—a child. She had chanced death to have it. And this was what she got. . . .

They took her back to her room. All that could be done for her had been done; but he could not leave her. Standing at her side, seeing the desolation in her face, he thought bitterly of the faith that had failed her. In spite of all her brave words and show of cheerful trust, she was no different from anyone else. Suffering had stripped aside all sentimentalities, and reality emerged: she was merely a mother with empty arms! And her mystic beads and sighing prayers were powerless to assuage the nameless anguish of that loss. . . .

He sat down at her bedside, his gaze never leaving her stricken face. Knowing the blighted wastelands through which she was walking, he felt he had a right to be at her side, for she had lost her child, and he had lost his love—

Sudden rage swept over him, the pain of his loss clogging his throat like a violent sickness, turning his whole being into such an unendurable futility that he wanted to curse aloud, to strike out, wildly—

Joyce's eyes had opened and met his. As swiftly as it had come, his unreasoning rage was gone. . . . She was in a worse condition than he: not only her mind was torn by anguish, but also her body—and suddenly, he wanted to reach out and, with one touch, take away all her pain. He wanted, for the first time to give . . . and he had nothing to give.

Her eyes, strangely still, were fixed on his, and although the surrounding flesh was still puckered tight with pain, the eyes themselves were quiet, deeply quiet, like the profound calm of some rock-sheltered pool of water, unmoving, untouched, although the sky was shuddering with tempestuous shocks of storm.

Wordlessly, she looked at him, unaware of the change that was coming over her. Gradually, her gaze seemed to lift and focus above and beyond him. Her lips were moving, but he could detect no word or sound. Intuitively, he sensed what she was trying to do—and the pitiableness of it was like a knife in his heart! The faith that had failed her, still held her in its coil: in the desert of her suffering, she groped towards a waterless oasis, a mirage, of her credulous imagination. . . .

Helplessly, he looked on, wanting to speak, and yet unable to: for he could only speak the truth, and the truth, at this moment, would be the ultimate cruelty. . . . And then, before his astounded eyes, he saw the thing happen: the blanched lips and pallid cheeks slowly suffused . . . not with any color, but with a softness, a peacefulness that was more breathtaking than great beauty. . . . It unfolded with the mysterious suddenness and slowness of a flower: one moment there was a tight, hard mask of pain, and then, in its place, there was this full-opened loveliness, this radiance of utter fulfillment. . . . Her lips kept moving slightly, but there were no words—only this aura of contentment, all about her, within her, engulfing her in its delight. . . .

A voice spoke, bewildered, husky with emotion: demanding, pleading with her to tell him what it was she was doing and saying. . . .

Her eyes rested on him, and there was a gentleness in her gaze beyond anything he had ever seen:

"Nothing," she said softly. "I am just holding on to God's hand."

He sat there, leaning slightly forward, expecting her to amplify. But this had not been the opening sentence: this was the entire mystery. . . . Abandonment—like a child to its father—confident that the mere expression of its dependence would cause His greatness to stoop to her littleness and obliterate the pain. . . . But it had not: she was still suffering. By all the laws of science she had to be; and his oblique suggestion of another hypo verified that fact. She did not need it. "The pain is different now. . . . *I don't mind it any more.*" She was above pain. . . .

In the dim light from the bedside lamp, he sat there, openly studying her face, waiting for he knew not what to happen. But there was no further change, only a deepening of this strange serenity that enfolded her. . . .

And after a long lapse of time, he began to speak again, stumblingly, with the awkward half-sentences and hesitancy of a child in its first day at school. His own confusion of pain and thwarted love had created an urgency and a need that brought with it a humility hitherto unknown. . . . And to all his forthright questions she gave answers, simply, clearly, with the vivid sureness of a child to whom its world of make-believe is actual and real. . . .

And when she was finished, he stood up and went from the room, her incomprehensible words filling his mind with a baffling sense that his hands were about an object too big for his grasp. . . .

Chapter 17

FOR some time he stood outside Joyce's room trying to shake free from the spell her words had laid on him. It had been a startling occurrence: a glimpse into an undreamed-of world. And it disturbed him, more than he cared to admit; because for the moment he had no way to refute the things she had said. But what, he asked himself, was the need for him to refute her childish beliefs? All this was intriguing enough but irrelevant. It must not be allowed to distract him from the vital personal problem that still faced him.

He went to the telephone booth in the lobby, called Arnet and blurted out the whole story of Elaine's discovery of their

159

intentions and her determination to change doctors. When he was finished, Arnet remained silent, as though waiting some additional information. "Who," he finally asked, "informed Elaine of our intentions?"

It was a vital point, and in the absorption of his own outraged feelings it had eluded Gray. "I don't know," he confessed, "but I intend to find out."

"If that person talks to the hospital authorities—" Arnet left the sentence hanging ominously unfinished.

There was grim assurance in Gray's voice. "I shall find out who it is, and I'll silence him."

"Yes; of course." The cynical dryness nettled Gray, recalling as it did his previous, ill-founded sureness that he could make Elaine agree to their course of action.

"If you don't think I am capable of tending to this matter," he retorted stiffly, "I am ready to let you handle it."

Arnet's flurry of excuses and advice did not placate him. With a cold word of farewell he hung up the receiver. He had expected constructive assistance rather than a fearful recommendation to be cautious. What place could caution have now in his actions? He was committed to an all-out attack.

A nurse glided past cradling carefully a prepared hypo in her palms; a technician, with her medical tray, came out of a room; a doctor stamped along at the side of a surgical cart. . . . This was the factual hospital world he knew: efficient, coördinated, emotionless. He had always felt at home in it, had considered himself a part of it. But this hospital was different, and its difference antagonized him. Outwardly the routine was the same, but beneath it there was a spirit as all-pervasive as air and as unyielding as rock. Yet, for the most part, it was a hidden thing, its manifestations slight, almost negligible—a word, a glance. Like Sister Liboria's moment of prayer that night in the emergency room, after the woman had died; like Joyce's words just now, intriguing, incomprehensible:

". . . Because He loves you He permits suffering to come—" (This was not love; it was a distortion of love. True love acts differently: the one I love I'll keep free of suffering —at any cost.) "But you are not the lover—He is. . . . And He has to make the one He loves lovable—" (Must he destroy whatever *He* thinks unlovable? What an intolerant Lover! . . . Devoid of all tenderness and sympathy.) ". . . You have to submit to a lover to know what He and His love are like—somehow, by suffering and sorrow—"

A disturbance at the far end of the corridor broke the trend of his thoughts. Two nurses were wheeling a shrouded cart into the elevator. He recognized Sandra; and dimly, like a ghost image, the memory of Clayton's death passed through his mind. Oddly enough the one detail that seemed of importance at the moment was that he had left his jacket in the room. . . . He stopped to retrieve it. Absentmindedly he thrust the bundled up jacket beneath his arm and continued towards his room. . . .

All of Joyce's fantastic statements added up to one word: submission. . . . What you could not understand or escape, you submitted to: hiding your head in the sand, escaping reality by investing unpleasant facts with a pleasant unreality of your own making. He halted: it had not been what Joyce said that had impressed him, but what her belief had *done* for her. . . . Facts, he never blinked; and the strange serenity which had lifted her above her pain, was a fact. But it had a number of explanations: the motor-power of the idea, self-hypnosis—the psychology books had lucid and lengthy explanations for it. It was not his province to decide the exact label which explained her behavior; nor was it necessary for him to do so. There was another fact that reduced the significance of this occurrence to nothing: *Her belief had not been able to save her.* . . His hands, his skill, his determined will had brought her through alive. That was a fact no one could escape. . . . The child? Well, its death was not his fault—she should never have tried to have a child in the first place.

The sight of the chaplain brought him to a sudden standstill. What was the man doing in front of his room? If he had come about Elaine— The same sudden fury of impotent anger that had overcome him in Elaine's room again swept over him. In this man all of the hospital's maddening influence stood embodied; and at that moment, if the chaplain had merely mentioned Elaine's name he would have felt the full force of Gray's violence and hate, regardless of consequences.

But the chaplain had come on another errand: he was worried about Clayton. The nurses had not been able to give him the information he wanted so badly. Certainly the farthest thing from his mind was to quarrel with the designs of

God—it was only that—well— "Didn't he ask for the priest? . . ." he ventured. "Wasn't there something . . . that he said . . . a request . . . maybe a question?"

"Nothing," replied Gray curtly. "Clayton said nothing. . . . If he did, none of us heard it." What was he so concerned about? The sorrow in his eyes—you would think he had lost his own brother. . . . But if even Father Chriswell had wanted to, he could not have enlightened Gray. For it was at that moment, and only then, that it had come home to him, with startling clarity, just what it was he was seeking. . . . And his miserable self-conceit, in wanting the triumph of his vicarious suffering blazoned forth by Clayton's open and full acceptance of the truth, humbled him wordlessly to the dust. . . .

The expression on Father Chriswell's face held only one meaning for Gray; and he hated him at that moment for trying to palm off on him another one of his psychopathic bits of play-acting. His hate made him rude. He stood rigidly before his door, making no gesture of invitation. And Father Chriswell, sensing his coldness, turned away, murmuring a word of apology for disturbing him. . . .

Gray watched the dark figure go slowly down the corridor and merge with the shadows. He found no satisfaction in the chaplain's evident dejection: it fell so far short of what he deserved. And for one mad moment Gray cursed the research which had tied his hands, and let this man again escape him. . . . But the hard fierce hate within his heart had a certainty

163

all its own: the time would come when this man, whose meddling interference had exposed Elaine to death, would feel the full force of his retaliation.

When he stepped into the room and tossed his jacket on the bed, it spilled open, exposing the crumpled up piece of evidence. For a moment he stared at it, and his lips twisted ironically. There was quite a bit, after all, that he could have told the chaplain about Clayton! This piece of scorched linen, accompanied by a word of explanation—and Father Chriswell would blacklist Sandra in every hospital in the state. . . . Perhaps he should have spoken. His condemnation of Sandra's conduct had not altered; but in view of what had happened to himself, it had lost its urgency. It was something to be attended to at a later date. . . . He crowded the scorched sheet into a drawer and dropped his jacket into the laundry hamper.

It was past midnight. His shift was ended, but there was no thought of sleep in his mind. He lit a cigarette and began pacing up and down the room. . . . He made no attempt to bring coherence into the events which had struck him like a swift staggering succession of blows. Everything was swallowed up in one inescapable fact: there was nothing left to him . . . except the research. In the face of that fact Arnet's warning, about the identity of the informer, suddenly took on a burningly sharp importance. Who was this person who held in his hands the one thing left him? . . . Step by step, he began to retrace his actions and words: There had been the meeting between himself and Arnet, in his house. There had been the phone call— His hand became aware of the small hard object it was nervously fingering. He pulled it out and stared at it—a gold and white pin, a nurse's pin. Irritably, he thrust it back into his pocket, unreasonably angered at these inconsequentials which kept intruding so persistently and inopportunely upon him and his personal problems. . . .

Chapter 18

"I FEEL that you yourself, if placed in a similar situation, would find this the only right and reasonable thing to do. . . ." There was the slightest of pauses, but the Chief-of-Staff merely nodded corroboration. "On all counts a change of doctors is indicated," Gray went on, "and both Elaine as well as myself would consider it a personal favor if you would take charge of her." He paused. "I have already informed Dr. Arnet," he added.

Throughout Gray's glib recital Dr. Bromwell had only spoken once, and that had been to murmur an agreement to the statement that "internal medicine was not Dr. Arnet's field." If he wondered why Gray, knowing that, had engaged

Dr. Arnet's services, he gave no sign of it. Now he signified his readiness to accept Elaine's case and his intention to study the reports at once: "The cardiac condition, I need not tell you," he said, "will be the vital factor. . . ."

There was something strangely reassuring about Dr. Bromwell's stolid, unemotional attitude, and Gray took leave of him with a sense of a disagreeable task satisfactorily discharged. Ironically enough, this transferring of Elaine's case into Dr. Bromwell's hands had lifted Gray higher in the Chief-of-Staff's good opinion than ever before. . . . It is apparent, Gray told himself, that for some odd reason Bromwell thinks I changed doctors because I mistrust Arnet's ideas on medical ethics!

Remembering the revealing questions he had asked Joyce, Gray found it hard to maintain with her the usual brisk impartiality of the attending physician. The relationship between them had subtly altered, and he resented it, even though he himself had been the cause of it. "It was thoughtless of me," he said, in reply to her hesitant question, "to have allowed my curiosity to disturb you with questions at a moment like that. I should not have done it."

The evasion (for it was that) stopped effectively any further attempt on her part to re-open the discussion of yesterday; but the look in her eyes made him feel as though he had rebuffed the generous offer of a child.

What patient of his had ever shown any concern about him personally? And she, with the anguish of her loss still fresh upon her— There was a sort of greatness here, and his heart paid silent homage to it. Yet he took leave of her without having made any allusion to the beliefs she had tried to share with him in his moment of need. They no longer seemed worth bothering with. The ease with which he had handled Bromwell had given his self-confidence a much-needed fillip. After all, he told himself, even more critical cases than Elaine's had come through successfully. Bromwell, who was far more experienced in obstetrical work than Arnet, had shown no undue alarm. . . . At the moment he was more tormented by the desire to see Elaine than by the fear of losing her. Joyce was greatly responsible for that. Her thoughtfulness for him, despite her own suffering, made his thoughtless behavior towards Elaine seem something shamefully selfish and small. Until he had Elaine's forgiveness he could not feel right. Yet he was unable to bring himself to go to her. "It's not my pride," he told himself. "I know it isn't. . . ." He knew what it was, but he shied away from admitting it: there was a Gray Powers whom he had not known before existed—fearful, violent, liable to lash out uncontrollably and harm even the one he most loved. . . .

The phone on his desk rang and he picked up the receiver, automatically murmuring, "Dr. Powers speaking." His heart gave a sudden lurch of happy surprise; it was Elaine speaking: Had he seen Dr. Bromwell yet—and had the arrangements been made—satisfactorily?

He assured her that they had. Dr. Bromwell had agreed to act as her physician. She could rest easily now. . . . The words of reassurance suddenly died. She had wanted to know if "the arrangements had been made—satisfactorily?" . . .

Nothing was satisfactory until he knew the identity of the informer.

It took her a strangely long time before replying. "It was just a voice," she finally vouchsafed, "on the phone."

His disappointment was so sharp that it made him oblivious to the tinge of resentment in her voice. He had expected more precise information than this. Surely she must be able to add something more definitely helpful— She interrupted him. Dr. Bromwell had just entered the room, and she could not keep him waiting. . . .

He put down the phone. . . . The research meant nothing to Elaine. What her real reason had been in letting him arrange the change of doctors, he did not know—but it had not been to safeguard his position as head of the research. That he was sure of. "She hates the research," he decided. "She hates the time and attention I give it." Their previous unity of thought and ideals was gone. He wondered now if it had ever existed. This over-possessiveness of Elaine's could not be a recently induced change in her. It was too radical for that—it must be a permanent trait, and he had been totally unaware of it! Bitterly he told himself that it had taken years of intimacy to discover that they were utter strangers.

A dust devil was gyrating across the desert; a saffron plume of twisting, swirling sand. It moved slowly, drifting its fine particles of brown dust about stones and shrubs and deserted dwellings, shrouding their harsh contours, burying them beneath the obliterating dust. . . . In time, all of life's harsh happenings were hidden, healed and buried beneath the accumulation of other events. Yet he found himself wondering if what had happened to him these past days would ever be forgotten or ended. . . . There were, he knew, malignancies, hidden deep and buried in the body, and they remained immune to all healing. . . .

Evening had come on, and the room seemed dark and unfriendly. He snapped on a floor lamp. The photo of Elaine, atop his desk, seemed to jump to life: the lips slightly parted, the eyes gently smiling. . . . He could not tear his gaze away from it, and, morbidly, his imagination kept picturing for him how death would congeal all that loveliness into an expressionless mask.

He seized the picture in his hands; then, helplessly, let it fall from his fingers.

The room was stifling him. There was death in it, smiling up at him, arrogantly, from the photograph, taunting his helplessness. . . .

He flung open the door and went from the room, leaving the door wide open, the lights still burning. . . .

The roof of the hospital was deserted. A low-riding moon laid a broad swathe of ghostly light along the outer edge of the roof. All about him was vast space and quiet—the broad expanse of the desert's face mutely upturned to the silent sky —and the calm of the night enfolded him, flowed into him. . . . It was as though he had outstripped pursuit and emerged into a haven of untroubled peace. . . . The thought was strange: he had rather prided himself on never fleeing from anything. . . . But he could see the reason for the thought: misfortune had hounded him so persistently (since his appointment to the research) that it had almost assumed the dimensions of a personality—a malign personality, dogging his every step, thwarting every move he made. But here, close to the great realities of earth and sky, the unreal imaginings fled.

The opposite side of the roof was lined with cubicles for sun-bathing; heavy shadows stretched out from them. He had started forward, when he saw, in the deepest part of the shadow, the white of a nurse's uniform. She was moving towards him, speaking as she came:

"I was waiting—hoping— You come up here sometimes for a breath of air, and I—" She had halted on the edge of the shadow; and he remembered a dimly lit room, with her crouched against a wall in the shadows— Abruptly, his mood of quiet was completely shattered:

"What is it you want?" he asked

"My pin. . . ." She waited. "Will you give it back to me?"

In the bleak light his face seemed granite. And it was not her tragic desertion of Clayton that turned him pitiless, but the sudden unreasoning feeling that somehow all his own misfortunes stemmed from that evil event. . . . "You will never wear that pin again."

"Oh, please, please. . . . I've paid for what I've done: I've been punished—" Her voice broke slightly. "I'm sorry, desperately sorry—"

Regrets came easily enough when one's misdeeds were uncovered; but regret did not basically change a person. "You would do the same thing again, if it were a question of a man's life or your own sefish interests."

"It wasn't selfish, what I did—believe me, it wasn't."

"I'll believe that when you tell me whom you saw—and why you had to see him."

"I can't." Her voice rose, the desperation of a trapped animal in its tones: "I can't tell you— Believe me, just this once. . . . I can't—"

There was cold finality in the way he turned away from her. . . . Fearfully she hurried after him. "Where are you going?" she demanded.

Between tight lips he replied, "To the chaplain."

She stopped dead in her tracks: "Is there no pity in you . . . no heart?"

The distraught, horrified cry spun him about: "*You* ask me that? You, who killed a helpless man by your neglect?"

"You drove me to it." The words leapt forth as though some hidden evil had broken cover.

"I? I drove you to it?" He stared at her. "Are you out of your mind?"

She caught her head in both hands, and the words that tore from her lips were a cry of pain and hopeless defeat. "I love you . . . I can't help it . . . I love you."

The anguished cry, like a ruthless hand, dug into him and ripped, rendingly, every shred of superiority from him. He stood there, wordless, his arms hanging at his sides, no longer the judge looking down on a groveling culprit, but just a man faced with the humbling mystery of a woman's love.

For there was no escaping the heartsick hopelessness of her confession: it had the ring of truth in it; it was the truth— and he felt suddenly soiled and guilty, unaccountably guilty, for he had done nothing to foster this mad infatuation of hers. . . . Anger came up in him: that she should try to enmesh him in her twisted affections, that she should dare to attempt to steal what belonged to Elaine exclusively— "Why do you tell me this?"

Her hands had dropped to her sides, but she did not raise her bowed head. What was she waiting for? Did she think him a child? He knew her kind of "love"—with it others had "loved" his own father—to death! "Do you think with that word 'love' to blindfold me, to lock my lips. . . ."

Her eyes, stricken, bewildered, lifted to his face . . . as she asked herself if it were possible that this was all he saw in her profession of love—a cheap attempt to buy her silence. And she had thought him so understanding of the weakness of others! "I believed the things you told me. . . ." She spoke with a slow heaviness trying to make the words convey to him what now she feared they could not. "I tried to live them. . . . You had done so much for me. I—I loved you for that—I wanted to be like you—" His cool regard sent a twist of pain through her heart. "I couldn't bear to see you trapped —as I had been—by events, by evil. . . ." Not a vestige of belief or interest showed in his face, and suddenly a flaming madness swept her: nothing mattered any more except to hurt him as he had hurt her. "That is why I left my patient." His head jerked upright. "Does that surprise you?" She gave a short, bitter little laugh. "It shouldn't, now that you know how I feel about you." Her voice was like the thrust of a knife: "I phoned your wife that you planned to kill the child."

She caught the sudden swift intake of his breath, and savage satisfaction flooded her. The depth of his hurt was visible in the stupefied look that filled his face, in the wide-staring question in his shocked eyes.

"Because I loved you," she said with burning bitterness, and when the wounded, questioning look still persisted: "I wanted to save you . . . as you 'saved' me. . . ."

The first slash of a scalpel is too deep and swift for pain. That comes later. And it was coming upon him now, a mounting overwhelming fury of outrage and emotion.

"You lie! You wanted Elaine out of the way." His voice shook with passion as he flung names at her, ". . . Nothing matters to you . . . nothing . . . except to get what you want."

"Even as you."

His arm whipped back, the fist clenched—

If she had flinched or cried out, he would have struck her . . . but she stood there, *expecting* him to strike!

And it was that which held him. There was fear in her eyes, and yet a defiance: she *knew* he would strike her, and the action would be proof that he was what she had named him—she believed everything she said about him!

With an evident effort, he jerked himself about and walked away. At the parapet he halted, his back to her: "Elaine is not going to die." There was a hard grating finality in his voice. "I'll see to it that she doesn't die . . . if it's the last

174

thing I do. She will not die. . . . You, and all your twisted,
rotten, scheming plans, are going to achieve nothing—you
hear? . . . Nothing!"

It was a wild defiance, shouted not only at her, but at the
low-hanging stars and all the silent forces of the night
gathered about him and against him.

A breeze fingered his hot cheek, a cool breeze. . . . Why
didn't she say something . . . do something? The presence
of the silent girl, back there in the shadows, was an oppressive reality: somehow or other he had to disarm her, silence
her. . . . His self-conceit bled at the realization that this
horrible situation was of his own making. In his plans for obtaining the research he had used her . . . and all the time
she had been using him! . . . Creeping up on his blind side
(so she thought), his religious side, to insinuate herself into
his affections. The irony of it! She had thought to gain his
love by acting religious—the only element in Elaine's love
that he could not tolerate! The infatuated fool! Wanting to
"save" him, when she had in her hands the club to beat him
into submission. She had made her choice: but it had been
the wrong one! She still held the club, but it was a useless
one now. . . .

She made no move as he approached her. "We know where
we stand now," he said coldly. "I can speak plainly." He drew
a deep breath, then spoke slowly, stressing his words: "It
would be mutually disastrous if you or I were to tell what we
know." He paused to let the full force of the implication
sink in: she could ruin him professionally, as he could her.

175

It was a stalemate. "And that is the way it is going to be . . .
whether you like it or not. . . ."

She had nothing to say to that. What could she say? What
could she do? . . . Her greedy little desire for the respectability and security which the profession of a nurse contained
was a chain that she, could not break. . . .

Chapter 19

SECRETLY, Gray had always admired the décor of Arnet's luxurious home. The old Spartan had surprisingly good taste: every item was genuine and exquisite. Gingerly, he touched the tips of his fingers to a gleaming black cloisonné vase, then stood back to admire it, feigning an interest he did not feel at the moment. . . . His recital of the encounter with Sandra had failed to elicit any comment. Arnet sat straight in his chair maintaining a judicial silence. All in all, Gray's own thought on the matter was that he had handled a difficult situation remarkably well: he had discovered and silenced the informer. Both he and Arnet were safely out of a very dangerous imbroglio.

Arnet's incisive voice suddenly broke the silence: "Return the evidence you have against her." It was a blunt order. "And you had better do it at once," he added.

Gray turned and stared at him. Arnet was in a foul mood he knew—but had he taken leave of his senses? The brooding way he kept looking at his hands told him that the rheumatoid condition was making itself distressingly evident. That would account for his grumpiness, but this . . . this insanity!

"There is no other way," stated Arnet stubbornly. "She will not trade her silence for yours—not this girl, believe me." But that was just what Gray could not do: believe him. "A show of generosity on your part may restore you in her eyes."

Gray did not want to be "restored" in her eyes: he wanted to ruin her for what she had done to him and Elaine. Circumstances, he admitted, made that, for the time being, impossible; but as soon as Elaine was out of danger he would find a way to settle accounts with Sandra.

Gray's arrogant cocksureness started a slow-burning anger in Arnet. Dourly he asked himself why he was bothering to advise him. His own medical career was ended. He knew that. The pain in his hands was quieted for the moment (he had attended to that), but the cause was still virulently active. His career was ended, but his pride rebelled that it should end with the stigma of what this hospital considered unethical conduct. "This girl still has the power," he growled, "to ruin us. She is going to use it . . . when she wants to." He fixed Gray with a mordant glance. "Your timetable, you know, is not going to influence her decisions."

Gray shook his head. "Her job means too much to her. She will do nothing to jeopardize that."

That arrogant assurance again! It was utterly destroying Gray's judgment. "Haven't you ever heard of 'the woman scorned'? . . . Don't smile! It's not a romantic fiction: it is a very unpleasant reality. . . . And this girl is more than that. She is a woman betrayed!" He paused and fixed Gray with a heavy glance: "Or don't you think she would have reason to consider herself such?"

It was hard for him to admit that, openly. Yet, if Sandra had taken as gospel the things he had told her (and she had stated very bitterly that she had) then he must have become for her the little tin god in her world of make-believe. . . . The emergence of his true identity destroyed the center of her world, making her life a mass of rubble. Oddly enough he understood that very clearly because Elaine had done a similar thing to him. . . . "I am practically certain," insisted Arnet, "that her job means nothing to this girl any more. She is interested in only one thing: retaliation—on you."

Suddenly thoughtful, Gray looked at him: "You think that? . . . You think she would throw overboard her professional reputation, her livelihood—just to get back at me?"

"And"—Arnet was emphatically sure—"count it a small price."

A vague uneasiness went through him. Arnet's opinion accorded uncomfortably well with what he knew of Sandra. There was in her that hard core of blunt recklessness. Perhaps he had been wiser than he knew in coming directly to Arnet—but the older man's advice still was absurd, a preposterous gamble. It would place both of them completely in this girl's hands.

"We are at her mercy anyhow," pointed out Arnet. "Right now your evidence against her is valueless; much more so later on if you attempt to use it. . . . Hasn't it occurred to you? . . . They will want to know why you did not accuse her right after the incident happened! Awkward, isn't it? . . . No matter what sort of explanation you dig up, your delay in reporting the affair is going to add credence and weight to her accusation of you. . . . No, no—this is the one and only way. Her infatuation for you isn't dead. Give it the merest gesture of good will and she will die rather than breathe a word against you. . . ."

The mere thought of speaking to Sandra again brought on an uncontrollable repugnance. Yet the more Gray thought of it, the more sensible did Arnet's views seem. Sandra had tried to save a life, and by so doing had killed a man: she had balanced a child's life against a worn-out, useless old man's life; and she had decided in favor of the child. . . . "No," he told himself, "that is wrong: she would not think that way." She knew enough about religion now to understand that *all* life is sacred to them; and she had been trying to act on religious motives. Her only thought would have been to save a child's life and avert a crime. . . . Clayton completely narcotized, would not have seemed endangered by a few minutes absence. . . . Distortedly, she had thought to do Gray a favor. What an egregious blunder that had been! And yet he had to concede that she had, in her way, wanted to do him a good turn. She must be sick with guilt at the way things turned out. . . . To return the incriminating evidence to her would not necessarily mean that he condoned her misdeed: it would merely indicate that he understood and was making allowance for her mistaken motives. And he, after all, was the only one who could straighten out her confusion and allay her guilt. . . . The more he thought of it the surer he became that Arnet was right. The stalemate would not last. Sooner or later Sandra would break out into action, disastrous action. There was only one way to silence her. Arnet's way: bring her over to his side. If she had gone overboard on the things he had told her he could restore her to reality. The generosity of his gesture would show her that greatness did exist, outside of the shadowy religious realm. . . .

Sandra's gaze took in every detail of the office. It was tastefully and expensively furnished, the last word in modern equipment. Her eyes gave no indication of the hate she felt, singly and collectively, for all this bric-a-brac, which the man she loved had schemed and lied and played with people's hearts in order to obtain. . . . He was seated behind the desk, an air of distinction exuding from him, newly shaven, resplendent in a becoming gray business suit. The big executive! . . . with the desk's broad expanse before him like an uncharted world to conquer. . . .

At his invitation, she settled easily in a chair, letting his opening remark about "some unfinished business between us" go unanswered. Her silence made him ill-at-ease; so she remained silent.

Nervously he toyed with a letter-opener. This self-possessed Sandra was a different sort of person. Vaguely he began to wonder if he had not been a fool to take Arnet's advice. He glanced up suddenly and surprised a look of such cold contempt in her eyes that it shocked him. Swiftly it was gone, replaced by the same cool indifference as before.

He cleared his throat nervously, pulled out a drawer and took a paper-wrapped parcel from it. He placed it on the desk in front of him. "I think," he said, "we both said things, the other night, that we would like to recall." The faintest spark of interest showed in her eyes. "It happened very suddenly," he offered, "and I think, to a great extent, we were both the victims of that suddenness." A smile would have helped the words achieve their purpose, but this small friendliness was beyond his power at the moment. "We are adults, and there is no reason why we can't act as adults. Under the stress of emotion I probably didn't behave very sensibly. I intend to repair that mistake now." The flicker of interest had gone from her eyes; she was watching him warily. He pushed the package towards her. "Take it," he said. "Destroy it." Her eyes were suddenly sharp, questioning. He nodded assent: it contained what she thought it did—the evidence of her dereliction of duty. "I have revised my previous opinions about the matter," and he finally managed the ghost of a smile. But she sat like a thing of stone, her hands in her lap. "It could cause you a great deal of trouble," he reminded her.

She was behaving very strangely. Her head turned slightly and she seemed to glance at one object after another, appraisingly, as though inventorying the contents of the room.

DARK ENEMY

Her gaze came back to him, held his a moment; then she stood up, turned, and started towards the door . . .

"Sandra!" She slowed her step, but did not halt. "Wait. . . ." She turned slowly as he came around the desk towards her. "That wasn't all," he hurriedly explained, and thrusting his hand into his pocket he found what he sought. She did not move as he extended his hand. He opened his fingers and the small gold object in his palm glinted in the light: "I'm returning your pin, Sandra," he said.

Swift as a striking snake, she moved. There was a flat dry sound as her hand hit his, violently . . . and then a small lost sound in the far corner of the room, marking the place where the pin had fallen. . . .

Stunned, he watched the door close on her, and a chill, numbing fear seemed to gather about his heart. . . . Dazedly, wonderingly he realized that she no longer cared about her job. . . . "I've got no way to keep her from talking!" She had not said a single word, but that significant stare of hers, taking in, tallying the contents of the room, had spoken more clearly than words: to get this fine place he had used her, deceived her; this then was her enemy, because this was his love. So she would take it from him, destroy it. . . . There was nothing he could do to stop her. She knew that. Why had she not done it already? Knowing from her own experience the anguish of awaiting an impending, unescapable disaster, was it her intention to subject him to that cruelty, too?

He sat there in the midst of what his ingenuity had won

and knew he had lost it. To have greatness in his hands, and then have a warped woman snatch it from him! . . . What dark malignancy was at work against him? Twisting people to its purpose, thwarting everything he tried to do? First, Elaine; then Sandra. Elaine, so good; Sandra so evil—and between those two forces of good and evil he was caught, and ground into dust. . . .

The intercom made a buzzing sound. Dully, Gray lifted his head from his hands and mechanically flipped the switch. "Dr. Bromwell to see you," announced the receptionist. Scarce knowing what he did, he muttered assent. . . .

The Chief-of-Staff came in briskly: the matter he had to discuss would require only a few minutes— He suddenly interrupted what he was saying. For a long moment he studied the expression on Gray's countenance; then he came towards him: "What is it, Gray? Worried?" he asked. "About Elaine?" Gray did not need to reply. Bromwell knew he had touched on the source of his despondency. "Her condition doesn't warrant pessimism," he encouraged. "She is doing nicely." Gray was glad to hear him say that. "But," he felt forced to explain, "there are some factors—some elements—" Bromwell had drawn up alongside the desk and placed a hand on his shoulder. "I know," he said, his voice low with understanding and sympathy: "It was a hard decision to make; and at times you must wonder whether it would not have been wiser to take the easy way. But you did make the decision—and it was the only right one." There was undisguised admiration in Bromwell's eyes. Gray turned his head; admiration would change to contempt when the Chief-of-Staff knew the truth. . . . But Bromwell solicitously persisted. "You know well enough *your* attitude is of importance, too. There is a sort of strength that comes from another's confidence—"

Gray nodded assent. He knew. That had been more than half the victory in Joyce's case: her confidence in him. . . . Secretly, he was aware that he could help in a way Dr. Bromwell would never dream of. A show of agreement with Elaine's ideas, with the reasons for her decision would mean a lot to her right now—it might be the one needed little touch to tip the scales in her favor. . . . "It is so important," explained Bromwell, "that she be kept quietly confident, her mind free of any worry. . . . I want you to spend as much time as possible with her, even if it means neglecting your work here. Your assistants can carry on temporarily. After all, you have a definite line mapped out for the research work. . . ."

He had, a very definite one—the one clearly and thoroughly outlined in his father's notes—and that fact kept coming back persistently after Dr. Bromwell had left the office. And gradually it emerged in its true importance. It was one of those fortuitous happenings, those casual remarks, fated to be a turning-point in a person's life. . . . Slowly, inexorably the elements of his decision formed and fell into place. . . . In a tight situation, Gray reminded himself, there is only one hope left a man: face the facts. One had to be a realist at all times, but utterly so when one's dearest possession was at stake. The research was lost—he would resign from the research! Ostensibly for Elaine's sake; actually to forestall

Sandra and make her victory an empty one. The research would continue to use his father's notes, with the understanding, that, when the time arrived, proper acknowledgment would be made, financially and publicly. . . . It did not require much imagination to visualize how the world at large would regard his resignation when they knew that it had been made for the sake of his wife. . . .

He took up his pen and began to write. Elaine's recent show of resentment for his attachment to the research was very vividly before him at that moment. "She will know now," he said resolutely, "once and for all. . . ." This, his resignation, would be conclusive proof that neither his work nor his plans for greatness were a rival to his love for her. . . .

Chapter 20

ARNET was unimpressed. He finished reading the document and placed it on the table before him. "Your singular originality," he said, in caustic reference to Gray's method of obtaining the research, "seems to be having singularly unoriginal results." He tapped the document with a long index finger. "You may have forgotten that I advised you to do this very thing—some time ago."

"There was no need of it then," countered Gray quickly. "Now there is. Elaine's condition has altered the picture."

With weary cynicism Arnet looked at him. "Another lady," he goaded, "has also had a share, I believe, in 'altering the picture.'"

Gray flared up. Was he supposed to be able to foresee the irresponsible way a psychopathic female would act? . . . What normal person would act as Sandra had? . . . This hospital was a natural sort of breeding-ground for this type of behavior—

Arnet's dry rejoinder, that since Gray had fed the flames he should not shout condemnation of the blaze, momentarily silenced him. "I didn't come here for a post-mortem on my conduct," retorted Gray sullenly, picking up his resignation and placing it in his pocket. He had expected at least a token sign of gratitude. After all, by surrendering his position as head of the research he effectively silenced Sandra, and so made Arnet's position permanently secure. . . .

But gratitude was the farthest thing from Arnet's mind. Gray had not told him about the secret arrangement he intended making with the hospital regarding his father's formula, but Arnet shrewdly suspected that Gray had, in some devious way, taken care of his own interests.

"She wants her pound of flesh," Arnet observed, "and you can't do anything but give it to her." His cold blue eyes glinted cynically. "But is the flesh going to be from the place nearest your heart?"

Gray stood up. "Regardless of what you think, Elaine is my main consideration in this." He told him then of Dr. Bromwell's recommendation, but the things which might have convinced Arnet he could not mention. Elaine's resentment of the research Arnet might believe, but not that the cause of it was her overpossessive love. Arnet thought Elaine was perfect.

I know, Gray told himself as he took leave, that my resignation is a surrender to this overpossessiveness of Elaine. But that means nothing to me, not a thing—if it will help her. . . . And she needed help. She had found nothing in her religious beliefs to help her, certainly nothing like what Joyce had found. All that she had derived from them had been that curious reversal of attitude, casting aside her dependence upon him; clinging stubbornly to a decision that held possible tragedy for both of them. . . .

He had expected reserve, a small hurt coldness at first; and he was prepared to be patient. But the eager way she called out his name, as he entered her room, brought him quickly into her arms. Her voice, slightly breathless with happiness, made no secret of her feelings. "Oh, I've been waiting . . . and waiting. . . ."

"I could not come sooner. . . . I wanted to," he stumblingly explained, "but I was so . . . so empty-handed."

"It was just *you* I needed," she murmured contentedly in his ear.

The words sent a warm little thrill through him. This was as it had been: himself holding first place in her affections. A sudden fierce joy shot through him at what he intended to do. The research was a bauble that he tossed willingly aside, for love of her. . . .

He sat at her side, and his heart was full with the greatness of this sacrifice he wanted to make for her. But no words would come. It was as though he had been away on a distant voyage, and the strangeness, resulting from that absence,

189

had first to be dispelled by silence before the intimacy of speech could again flow freely.

She reached forward suddenly and took his hand. In his softened mood the little gesture was eloquent of a love that had never wavered. And he saw the disastrous conflict that had arisen between them as the result of their failure to understand each other. How could a man and woman share their deepest thoughts and longings, and yet know so little of each other? "Do you think, dear," he asked, "that I am the sort of person who would oppose the truth . . . the real truth?"

"No, Gray," she answered quickly, "I know you wouldn't." Her eyes lifted to his. Their problem had not been as simple as that. "What you believed truth was falsehood to me—what was I to do? To yield would have been treachery to myself . . . to you . . . and our love. . . ."

Gently, he asked: "Has compulsion any place in love?"

"Oh, my dear," she protested, "love itself is a compulsion, is it not? My love for you forced me to protect the fruit of our love." He sat there, thoughtfully, saying nothing. "Don't you understand, dear?" she pleaded.

His gaze settled on the small hand holding on to his own so trustingly, and he thought of Joyce. . . . Perhaps a person's beliefs could have much more effect on illness than he had realized. He wanted to believe that now; he had to believe it. If it could do for Elaine what it had done for Joyce— "Yes; I do understand, Elaine," he said, "because, you see, I have learned a number of things these past days—" His eyes came up to meet hers. "You did the right thing, Elaine—I know that now, because I know and agree with the reasons that lay in back of your decision."

Her arms were suddenly about him: "Oh, I knew you would!" she exclaimed happily. "I prayed so hard. . . ." Her cheek was pressed against his and so she did not see the expression that flickered across his face.

After a while she drew her head back, and when he saw how her whole countenance was transfigured, he turned aside, unable to look upon the miracle of happiness his deception had worked.

But she put her hand lightly against his cheek, and turned his face towards her. She studied him with that frank, lingering look he knew so well. "There is something—" she wondered softly. ". . . You seem sort of . . . different. . . ."

His quick little smile held faint embarrassment. "No, dear, not different—just repentant." His attempt to ask forgiveness, she brushed aside.

"It's all over and forgotten, Gray," she assured him.

Doggedly, he shook his head. "It isn't—it can't be—not while the cause of it is still there. . . . It will be a wall between us, a wall that has to come down—" She was looking at him in open puzzlement: "You know what I'm talking about, don't you?" She shook her head. "The research."

"Oh, no Gray. There is nothing I want you more to have—" His look halted her momentarily. "Really, dear, it is the truth. It is *our* dream come true."

Her face was radiant. She was glorying in the research; it was a crusade for limitless good; something to achieve; something to live for!

A sickening sense of futility shot through him: everything he attempted to do or plan—

There just seemed to be no pattern of human behavior that had any consistency in it.

He leaned forward to hide from her the beaten, defeated look that he could not keep from showing in his face. His head was inclined, making a pretense of regarding with loving absorption the hand he held in his. As he moved slightly, adjusting his position, the envelope in his pocket made a small muffled crackling sound, reminding him, maddeningly, how closely he had come to doing Elaine harm instead of good. . . .

Her voice was a murmur of soft sound. . . . As from a far distance, he caught the little phrases, the daydreamy tones of her voice. . . . It was a return to an appealing little game of their childhood days: she was building a world of make-believe with him in its center. Only now she was dreaming of the research as a kingdom, with him ruling it, wisely, simply, nobly, every word and gesture and act befitting his parentage, great as his father had been great; giving himself, unstintingly, as his father had done—achieving greatness by laying aside his own littleness, getting outside of himself by giving unsparingly of himself, even though all the rest of the world kept greedily, blindly taking, taking. . . .

Her voice died away into silence: and he made no effort to reply . . . because, for one enchanted moment, he was back again in a long-forgotten world, where dreams were the abiding realities, and reality just a passing dream. . . .

Chapter 21

THE address, which Sister Felicita had obtained for Gray, turned out to be a tiny white box of a cottage. Oleander bushes, limp for lack of water, hedged in the approach, and a seedless mulberry tree spread its shade over a struggling attempt at a cactus garden. He threaded his way down a flagstone path and pressed the button at the side of the door. The blinds were drawn on the windows, and he had begun to fear that she might be away for the day when the door swung open.

At sight of him, Sandra's face froze. She started to swing the door shut, but Gray's broad shoulder suddenly thrust forward: "You must give me a few minutes—please." And when she still resisted, he pushed his way forcibly past her. Stiff with anger she faced him. "Forgive me," he pleaded, "but this is so important—I *must* talk to you."

She did not want to hear him, no matter what he had to say. Nothing he could say could add to what she already knew. She had crossed to a studio couch and sat down on its edge, her back to him. . . .

"I'm not here to talk about myself," he said humbly. Sandra leaned over and snapped on the radio. "It's my wife I want to talk about. . . . Elaine—" A surge of music from the radio drowned out what he was saying.

He crossed the room and snapped it off. In a swift violent movement Sandra came to her feet—she was close up against him, and he made as though to put a quieting hand on her shoulder. But she flung it aside, and stood glaring at him.

"I'm sorry," he said contritely, "I had no right to do that. . . ." He stood there, waiting for her anger to abate. "I know how you feel about me, and I'm not asking you to change that. But my wife hasn't harmed you. . . . She is completely innocent. . . . What you intend doing to me may make all the difference whether she lives or dies. . . ." He could not control the slight trembling that had come into his voice: "You see the research means a great deal to her—" He broke off, unable to continue, his heart turning sick at the sudden satisfaction showing in her face.

"Go ahead," she prompted. "I'm a good listener—or have you forgotten. . . ."

He took that: it was due him. . . . "I tried to make up for that," he reminded her, his voice very low, "but I'm not trying

that any more. I don't want anything for myself. . . ." Her
eyebrows lifted skeptically. "It's the truth . . . it's only
Elaine I'm thinking of. . . ."

He told her then how he had gone to Elaine with his resignation, and how he had realized, almost too late, that the
loss of the research would be a blow to her. In her precarious
condition everything counted. He *had* to retain the research—
for her sake. From his pocket he drew an envelope: "Here it
is . . . my resignation. . . . If you will just wait until Elaine
is out of danger—"

She put the back of her fingertips against his extended
hand and flipped it aside: fairy-tales did not interest her any
longer. She walked to the door and held it open. "How you
intend to do it, I don't know. But one thing I am very sure of:
you are not giving up what you wanted so badly that you lied
and cheated—"

"But my resignation—"

"Doesn't mean a thing," she cut in, "to me! With Elaine out
of danger you could be *'persuaded'* to revoke your resignation."

He went past her, his hands still holding the envelop, but a
strange fixity had come into his gaze, like a man walking in a
world gone suddenly dark. . . .

A rainstorm swept in from the west . . . sudden, violent . . . flinging drops of rain spitefully against the window-
panes. . . . It would be as brief as it was sudden. Rain came
rarely to the desert, and it seemed to want, by its violence, to
make up for its long delay in coming. . . . A shattering spear

of lightning lanced through the clouds, and in its bluish brilliance, all the outside void of blackness was momentarily illumined: the distant, dark mountains, the shining wet ribbon of road, the dimensionless desert. . . .

Sandra's final words had been as startling and revealing— Gray turned away from the window. He dreaded the very thought of Sandra. Each new encounter with her was like another step down a stairway into an ever deeper darkness. She had lost everything; she had no faith in anything. *He* had been her faith, and he had failed her . . . and now, because of that, Elaine might die. . . . "You are not giving up what you wanted so badly that you lied and cheated—" Her ruthless clarity, at least, she had not lost. Although he had not told her all, she had sensed the truth. It was only the outward shell that he was parting with—not the reality. To restore her faith in him it would have to be all or nothing . . . the research, the formula, everything had to be surrendered. . . .

That was clear to him: academically clear; but it was utterly impossible. It would mean falling back into the herd of the nameless, the ordinary. . . . And he could never do that, because the desire for greatness was in his flesh and blood and brain. . . .

A tremendous clap of thunder startled him; shook him. Rain thrummed against the window as remorselessly as the thought which beat maddeningly in his brain: his ambitions had destroyed Sandra; by giving them up he (and he alone) could redeem her. He had taken, he must give: it was the pulse-beat of some cosmic justice, stating, demanding, insisting. . . . He fought the thought as though it were a living person. Fiercely he twisted and turned to escape it. He could not yield to this destruction of all his ambitions. He said it aloud, time and again . . . and suddenly, the picture Elaine had evoked stood again before him: the picture of a man whose life was a giving, not a taking.

He stood there in the rain-darkened room, and glimpsed only now what her words meant. Greatness was love, for love was a giving, an endless giving—and to Elaine love was inclusive, embracing everyone and their needs; but he saw it as exclusive, centered singly and absorbingly, on the person you loved. Elaine he loved; for her sake he must risk everything, expose himself to Sandra's humiliating accusations. "I would rather be dead," he told himself darkly, "than face this. . . ." The entire hospital would look on with morbid interest while he scrabbled frenziedly to hold onto his job. A nurse pillorying a doctor! The drama of it would set all tongues wagging. . . . He decided he did not care. "Let Sandra do her worst. I'll brazen it out somehow or other. . . . I simply have to hold on to the research—for Elaine's sake."

Chapter 22

THE clean, thin light of a new day filled the main office. The floor was newly swept, the woodwork and chairs had been carefully dusted, and a small vase of fresh flowers adorned Sister Felicita's desk.

She looked up and smiled a greeting at Dr. Powers. "In a moment, doctor," she assured him, and turned back to the record of admission she was making out.

He stood there, his face somewhat drawn, his shoulders slack. His eyes felt as though there were sand beneath the lids. He had not slept much last night.

Footsteps sounded heavily in the corridor. There was not much of a rhythm to them; it was merely the sound of a

number of people walking, going somewhere. He looked up.
The night shift was going off duty. He could see them go past
the corridor at the end of the lobby: young girls, blue capes
over their rumpled uniforms, tired, their eyes shadowed with
weariness. Tonight they would again go past that door, trim
in fresh white uniforms, well-rested, their eyes alert; but now
they walked with a stolid, weary purposefulness as though
there were nothing more desirable than untroubled rest and
sleep, away from the sick and suffering. . . .

During all the hours of the night, the hospital had functioned: ushering in new life, aiding the suffering through
hours of pain, assisting the dying over the dark threshold.
There was something elemental in its all-embracing compassion and unending care: something of the same passionless-
ness and purposefulness that characterized the earth with its
endless succession of seasons, the sea and its rhythmic ebb
and flow of tides. . . . Yet the distress that had kept him toss-
ing fretfully all night, the anguish of having decided and yet
being undecided, was a suffering the hospital could not touch
nor alleviate. It was beyond the hospital's scope. For the hospital's machinery of healing ministered to tangible suffering,
not the intangible—despite what this particular hospital
thought. . . .

Again the torturing indecision twisted through him; no
matter which way he turned he was guilty of a terrible wrong:
by being true to his love, he would be false to justice . . .
by doing the right thing to Sandra, he would do the wrong
thing to Elaine. The crossroads of decision had been reached
and passed. He had told himself that a thousand times, and

the sleepless hours of the night mockingly refuted that. . . .
In his confusion and utter weariness he was blind to what
would otherwise have been abundantly clear: this was not
just indecision; but conflict. Something deep within him was
struggling desperately to express itself; despairingly it fought
for its life—and the violence of its efforts overflowed into his
body filling it with a distress more acute than physical
suffering. . . .

The conflict he could escape under the cloak of indecision;
but the suffering he could not escape. . . . Where did you
go to escape what was inside of you? What did you do when
the suffering could not be touched with the hand or seen with
the eye? . . . When you could not trace it with the micro-
scope or laboratory tests? . . . What did you do?

He heard the voice over the intercom: the quiet, prayer-
ful voice of a Sister: ". . . I offer Thee my prayers, works,
joys and sufferings of this day. . . ." He had heard it so many
times: it was said each morning. ". . . For all the intentions
of Thy Sacred Heart, in union. . . ." The formula of words
had always been a vague, unmeaning sound to him, part of
this hospital's strange pattern of behavior; but suddenly, it
was the faith of Joyce speaking again to him, the faith of
Elaine, renewing its source of strength . . . and for a wondering moment he visioned those other sick and bedridden ones,
in private rooms and wards, repeating in their hearts these
words, which fused all those stricken bodies into a great
oneness of belief, as they faced another day of helplessness
with the corporate prayer of trusting hopefulness. . . .

Sister Felicita was speaking to him, and he turned slowly

to her. It took him a moment to remember what he had wanted to ask of her: an illustrated weekly wished to do a feature article on the research. They were sending photographers this morning. Would she call him when they arrived? He would be in his wife's room.

Sister Felicita made a note of his request, remarking casually that Elaine had not had a very good night. His look of evident alarm brought quick reassurance. "There was no need to call you doctor. . . . It was not that serious. She just seemed restless, unable to sleep—" She broke off her explanation: "All of the Sisters are praying, doctor," she confided sympathetically.

The genuine concern in her face had an odd effect upon him: What will she say? he wondered. How will she look at me . . . after she knows? He managed a shamefaced word of appreciation, then crossed the lobby to the elevator.

A fresh earth-sweet smell came through the open window. It was reminiscent of soft damp soil yielding to the thrust of tender green growing things. Last night's rain had injected a new verve into the garden. A whiplash of bird song, clear, challenging, cut the clean thin air, waking in Gray's heart, a memory of sun-dappled fields and of a pool of quiet water fringed with drooping willows. . . .

Springtide was again abroad in the world; and Elaine, reclining so quietly against her pillows, was somehow part of it. On her was the great quiet preceding the unfolding of new life, that mystic tranquility which surrounds and permeates the creative act . . . and he was powerless to restrain the

201

dull, unreasoning resentment which rose up in him against
the new life she held. For the bitter trials of the past days,
and his present crucifixion between ambition and love, would
never have come to pass if it had not been for the child. . . .

Elaine was looking at him, her eyes telling him how happy
she was because he was there. And it struck him, for the first
time, how like she was to Sandra: the dark hair and eyes, that
exquisite line of lip and feature— But no, he told himself,
they were worlds apart. Elaine's beauty was something inside
of her. . . . This present silence of hers was part of it. Instinctively she had sensed that he was troubled, and although
her own moment of crisis was hourly drawing closer, she
thought only of him, and waited the disclosure of his trouble,
so she could lighten or dispel it. . . . If only he could *do*
something . . . anything! She was so sweet and good—and—
"I love you, dear," the words spilled out, tremblingly low.
"I love you." A quick little light kindled, responsively, in her
dark eyes. "No matter what I've said or done or tried to do, I
love you. . . . It's a different love than before—maybe I
didn't really love you before, but now I do. . . . Nothing
can change that, nothing can add to it . . . nothing will—"

He plunged his head in his hands, his emotion choking
him. . . . And Elaine's hand drifted lightly over him, touching his hair, his cheeks, caressingly; telling him in love's wordless fashion that she understood and loved as deeply and
tenderly in return. . . .

They had been so far apart. . . . They had hurt each other
so deeply in spite of their mutual love. But it was no longer a
mystery to her why love should do this: by the things we

are hurt, by them, too, are we healed. What the future had
in store for her she did not know. She had seen clearly when
she made her decision that it could very well mean her life.
And she loved life—and there might be very little of it left to
her. . . . A heavy sense of responsibility still weighed upon
her: for, to her mind, it was on her that the guilt lay for many
of Gray's wrong notions. . . . "Gray?" she murmured gently,
and he lifted his head slowly, "if the worst should happen,"
she said, "and I—"

A look of fear jumped into his eyes. "I don't want you to
think of that, Elaine. Please. Keep that out of your mind . . .
completely. . . ."

Her glance was gentle with reproach. "You were always
the realist, Gray. Is this the time to change?"

Shamefacedly, he looked down at his hands, unable to
meet the challenge of her courage. Finally he mumbled a
reply: "Life would have no further meaning for me—if you
were gone."

Her eyes filled: "Oh, my dear, I know . . . and that is why
I am speaking. Suppose the child should live?"

"I could only hate it." She gave a little start of shocked surprise . . . and he could have bitten off his tongue for be-
traying him.

"You didn't mean that . . . did you, Gray?" A faint puzzlement marred the serenity of her face, for he had assured her
that her views were now his. "You couldn't," she went on a
trifle anxiously. "The child is our child—part me, part
you. . . . Our love lives on in the child."

He sat there, saying nothing, unutterably ashamed and

fearful lest his blundering speech again betray him and do her harm. And after a long wait he lifted his head and let her see the desperate contrition in his face. "I . . . I didn't know what I was saying," he admitted humbly.

But this time her love did not rush forward to brush aside his effort to make full amends. Silently she looked at him, and he knew she was waiting for him to unsay explicitly what he had said. But in spite of his love, the words came hard: "I'll take care of the child," he said, his voice very low.

She held his face between her hands and looked deeply into his eyes: "As your own father cared for you?" she pleaded.

His gaze flickered then steadied: " . . . I promise," he said.

She took him into her arms then, and her happy little sigh awoke in him a strange, swift tenderness. His arms tightened, gently, protectively about her, and all his confusion and fears, his vague self-reproach dropped from him. . . . Again it was springtide, and mysteriously they were together again at the edge of a tree-shadowed pool in their first April together. He had always kept that month in his heart, that month when overcast skies opened up to let forth gleams of sunlight, that month when the darkness of death yielded to the brightness of new-springing life. . . . And as she listened a gentle sadness touched her eyes, for she could only think of all the long years of barren happiness, before they had rediscovered the tear-wet smiles of April.

Chapter 23

IT WAS late the following afternoon when Gray's phone rang. Dr. Bromwell's voice was calm, unhurried, as though nothing out of the ordinary had occurred: "Her breathing is bad. . . . I don't think we should wait." Gray's hand tightened about the receiver. He had seen Elaine that afternoon, just a few hours ago. She had been perfectly all right— "We are taking her to surgery at once. . . . the child has a chance now, you know—in fact, to save the child we have to operate now—as well as to save the mother—"

"Hold everything," he broke in sharply. "I'll be there right away."

He was still some distance from Elaine's room when he saw that the door was open— Had the fools failed to wait for him? Was she as critical as that? He hastened into the room and brought up short: the attendants had just finished placing her on a surgical cart . . . a sheet was tucked about her; only her face was visible, and it was white and strangely different. . . . He bent down: "You want me to stay with you, don't you, dear. . . . Surely now—" She shook her head in refusal, but her eyes were fixed on his, petitioning something. . . . Swiftly, he bent lower and placed his lips against hers.

Her head turned slightly and she was whispering, urgently, in his ear: "Your promise, dear—you will keep it . . . won't you?"

For a split second he hesitated, not knowing what she was referring to: "I will," he assured her swiftly, "you know I will. . . ."

But she had caught the momentary hesitation: "The child," she reminded him, ". . . and all the other things—"

"I meant them," he lied. "I meant every one of them."

Her soft little sigh of relief merged into: "I love you, Gray," and then, against his lips: "Good-by . . . dearest. . . ."

"Not good-by," he said forcefully, "good luck."

Something strange seemed to shadow the depths of her eyes, something dark, hooded, premonitory . . . and her lips moved again, soundlessly, as though framing again that same word of farewell. . . .

A hand touched his shoulder, and he straightened up. Dr.

Bromwell's glance went past him and the attendants started moving the cart towards the open door. Involuntarily, he started after it, but the Chief-of-Staff's hand held him. . . . Resentment flaring openly in his eyes, he turned on the Chief-of-Staff, but the restraining hand did not release its hold: "I know," Dr. Bromwell said quietly. ". . . You want to be with her. . . ." Stolidly he shook his head: "She does not want you present. . . . She told you that before; and she just now confirmed it." He shrugged his shoulders slightly. "We don't understand these things . . . much less quarrel with them. We just do whatever makes it easier for her: even though it makes it harder on you. . . ." His hand tightened reassuringly upon Gray's shoulder, then fell away as he started towards the door.

Gray stood there, his arms hanging slackly at his sides. What Bromwell had said was just common sense, correct procedure; his own insurgent desires must be subordinated. "I'll be in my office, doctor," he called after Bromwell. "If you— that is, if there is any need—" He broke off abruptly, aware that he was blunderingly expressing a doubt of the other's ability.

Dr. Bromwell nodded understandingly: "I'll call you," he promised and went from the room. . . . After a moment, Gray followed him. . . .

The corridor was dim, and deathly silent. The nurses and Dr. Bromwell, grouped about the cart, were moving quietly, almost soundlessly down the corridor . . . away from him— and suddenly his vision blurred. Roughly, he swept the back of his hand across his eyes, once, twice, clearing his vision. . . . They were at the far end of the corridor now, and, for a moment, they stood still.

Helplessly, he watched them, knowing what they were about to do, yet unable to stop them. . . . The doors swung open, and a flood of radiance poured from the room into the corridor's dimness: it enveloped the still form on the cart and laid a shaft of light down the length of the hallway transfixing him where he stood. . . . It took but one sickening heartbeat of time—and then it was all over; the brightness had taken her in. . . . The doors swung shut, and he was alone: in a long emptiness of walls, closed doors, and silence. . . .

Something deep inside of him seemed to twist and break with sickening suddenness: and the pain of it was vaguely familiar, like something once experienced, causing him to stand there in the empty hallway, stricken and trembling. . . .

As on the dim edge of a dream, he heard footsteps, coming towards him. A nurse passed and glanced up at him. She stopped, took a step towards him, and her face seemed to materialize before him, a young face filled with grave concern. . . . He spun about on his heel and walked away, quickly, blindly, like a man fleeing. . . .

Night had come down peacefully over the desert. From his office window, he could see the lights of the town blinking across the dark, and each of them was a bead of remembrance. . . . His mind slipped from one memory to another, telling the rosary of their happy days together. And all the while he was fearfully aware that, if tragedy struck, this would be all that remained for such as he—memories.

Sick with apprehension as he now was, not knowing where to turn for help, it came clearly to him that it was Elaine who had always been his strength. Since that first moment, by the side of the pool, it was she who had smiled away all trouble or unpleasantness. The strength that was in her she had given to him. Never had she had to turn to him—except that one time: when her mother had died. . . . And he perceived now why that had been: he had established himself by then as the center of her life—she had traded allegiances—and he knew now that he had, unknowingly, harmed her. For what she had surrendered was greater than what he had given. The proof of it was here before his eyes: she had returned to her childhood faith, and in it had found the strength to meet this present ordeal quietly and unafraid. And, as before, she wanted to share that strength with him. That was what her words had meant, her reminder of the things they had spoken about. She knew how great a trial this was going to be for him, and she was trying to point out to him the source for help: her source . . . so that her strength would be his—

The phone rang shrilly, startling him. He ran across the room and snatched up the receiver: "Yes?" he asked breathlessly.

It was Sister Martha, profoundly apologetic: a boy had been brought in, with a badly burned hand, and she had been unable to obtain a doctor. Gray exhaled a huge sigh of relief. "It's all right, Sister. . . . I'll take care of it—but if Dr. Bromwell calls see that I get the message at once. . . . Don't delay on it, please. . . ."

It was a routine case. How many hundreds of these he had handled: burns, fractures, wounds. . . . And yet none of them had ever affected him as this one. The boy, still grubby from play, was trying so valiantly and vainly to hold back his whimpering cries. . . . But it was not that which affected him so deeply: it was the look in the boy's eyes: a look of stark, naked terror, horrible to witness in one so young. . . . And because the same terror, only greater, was in his own heart, compassion came up in him like a flood. "It's all right, son," he assured him, "it's all right . . . there's nothing to be afraid of. . . . You are not going to lose that hand. . . ."

Through his tears, trembling hope spoke: "For sure? . . . Honest?"

He smiled: "As sure as I'm standing here. . . ."

His touch had never been so soft, his voice never so gentle, lulling the boy's fears, keeping the young mind from attending to what he was doing. . . .

The Sister, who had been assisting, stood at his side, as he was scrubbing up afterwards: "That was wonderful, doctor," she said in a low aside.

A strangely satisfying little thrill went through Gray. He reddened slightly, not knowing what to say in reply. Finally he managed something about "just doing the job he was supposed to." Hurriedly, he dried his hands and went from the room.

More than once Gray's medical skill had elicited flattering commendation. He had grown used to it; he accepted it as a matter of course. Why should he now derive such satisfaction from a Sister's little word of praise for his *personal attitude* towards a patient? Had he been wrong all these years? A doctor was supposed to be impersonal. It was imperative that he be: pain was an enemy ruthlessly cold and emotionless, and a doctor was trained to be emotionless when he met it. . . . But now he suddenly realized the flaw he had allowed to creep into that essentially right attitude: he had fought suffering because he hated suffering, and not because he loved the sufferer—

He was passing the desk when the intercom suddenly spoke: "Dr. Powers . . . calling Dr. Powers. . . ."

In two quick strides he was at the desk, and had snatched up the phone. . . . He heard only the opening words: "This is very urgent, doctor. Dr. Bromwell requests—"

The elevator was in use—he bolted towards the emergency stairway. In great leaping strides he went up the stairs, frantic with the need to get to her, before it was too late. He had to get to her . . . in time. . . . "O God . . . give me time . . . let me get to her in time . . . don't let her die . . . don't—"

The sudden stabbing pain in his side choked off his desperate pleading—

Gasping, he came to the landing. The sound of his running footsteps filled the long corridor with empty, lost echoes. He flung wide the door. . . .

The nurses spun about as the door hit the wall. Quickly Dr.

DARK ENEMY

Bromwell started forward, but Gray's distended eyes did not see him. They saw only the figure in black, by the side of the table, and the small black book in his hands. . . .

Blindly, he went forward, shouldering aside the chaplain. . . . Her eyes were shut, her lips closed. . . . Tremblingly, his hand stole forward and touched her cheek: "Dearest . . ." he said brokenly, and waited. . . . But she did not answer. . . . She did not speak. . . .

Chapter 24

D EATH, which is an ending is also a beginning—both for
the one who has gone and for those who remain. But
for Gray, seated broodingly before Father Chriswell's desk, it
was exclusively an ending. The love that was his life was
irrevocably ended. All the things which he still had to say to
her would remain unsaid: the deceit he had practised on her
she would never be able to condone because he could never
explain now—she was gone. . . . And the words of sympathy
which Dr. Bromwell had spoken after accompanying him to
his room were empty sounds; the concern, the phrases of
medical explanation were all unrelated to him. They had
been for another person: a person who neither heard nor felt

any longer. Lost in the joyless vista of a life without Elaine, he was not even aware when Dr. Bromwell left him. There was only one reality and it was too vast for words, too deep for tears. . . .

As though it were burned into his brain, he saw again the silent whiteness of her upon that table of death, and at her side, in that last moment, the figure of the man who had brought her to that end.

A small hot flame of madness kindled in the midst of his black despair. . . . And it grew with a swiftly flaring intensity: a warmth in the frozen wastes of his heart. . . .

Like some mindless, instinct-driven creature, he had gotten to his feet and gone from his room. The chaplain's door had been open, a light burning on the desk. He walked in and knocked on the bedroom door. No one answered. He knocked again, loudly: but there was no response. The chaplain was out on a call. . . . Grimly he sat down at the desk, and here he would remain. This time there would be no escape . . . and, this time, no mercy. . . .

The thought never crossed his mind that what he was about to do would completely ruin his career. If it had, it would not have mattered. Grief had partially unhinged him; and all that mattered was to wreak vengeance upon the one who had inflicted this intolerable suffering upon him. . . .

A small cardboard box was on the desk top close to his right hand. Mechanically, he pushed it aside. With sightless absorption he stared at the book lying open beneath the desk lamp. . . . Quietly, peacefully, a wall clock kept ticking off the seconds in the silent room; and, by slow steps, the letters on the page before him became words, a group of words, sentences, heavily underscored in pencil:

"So they came to Mara, and even here they could not drink the water, so brackish it was to the taste; it was with good reason he called it Mara, for Mara means Bitterness. Here the people were loud in their complaints against Moses: What shall we do for water? they said.

"Whereupon he cried out to the Lord, and the Lord showed him a tree whose wood turned the waters sweet when it was thrown into them. . . ."

As through a blood-red mist he saw again the square-shouldered figure standing by the side of Elaine's lifeless body, untouched by the tragedy his poisonous ideas had wrought.

Sudden fury brought him to his feet, wild-eyed, shaking with a passionate urgency to cut this man's monstrous arrogance to ribbons. . . .

The shrill clangor of a phone spun him about. . . . The sound was coming from the bedroom. Scarce aware of what he was doing, he crossed the room and jerked open the door.

The bedroom was empty; the bedclothes flung back in disorder. . . .

Abruptly the phone stopped ringing.

For a moment he stared at the silent instrument, then suddenly snatched up the receiver: "Dr. Powers speaking." His voice was hard, tight, relentless. "Locate Father Chriswell . . . I have to speak to him . . . at once . . . in his office. I'm waiting. . . ."

215

He gave the receptionist no chance to reply: at the moment she did not exist. No one existed, except this man, this person of evil, whom he had to destroy. . . .

He was crossing the room when he saw it: a cumbersome object draped across the back of a chair. The sight of it seemed to root his feet to the floor. . . . Almost fearfully he put forth his hand and touched it. It was real. With distended eyes he examined it: it was not new; it had been used a great deal. The brace slipped from his fingers to the floor. . . .

Slowly, as though he had no will in the matter, he went back into the study, crossed to the desk, and picked up the small cardboard box. He took out one of the tablets and put it to the tip of his tongue. Woodenly, he stared at the name on the box: Bromwell would not have prescribed this unless there was pain, plenty of pain. . . .

A slight sound caused him to turn. The priest was standing just inside the doorway, and in the dim light he seemed fantastically changed. He was formless and stooped, sick and old; and there was a trace of breathlessness in his voice when he spoke: "I got here," he apologized, "as quickly as I could."

And he had not stopped, as was his custom, before the door in order to call up those mysterious, hidden reserves of courage he possessed. Another's need brought him running, his own suffering forgotten—and this was the arrogance he wanted to cut to ribbons!

The deep-set eyes were looking at him, intently, anxiously: "You did want to see me, didn't you, doctor?" he urged.

"Yes," he replied, "I did. . . . I wanted to ask you a question." Readily, the priest started forward into the room. "But it's too late now."

Father Chriswell halted: "Too late?" he echoed blankly.

"Yes . . . I've got my answer."

With frightened eyes the chaplain watched Gray go past him. He had seen that blank stony look before, on the faces of the despairing and the lost. . . .

Chapter 25

SHE lay on the bed, her hands on top of the counterpane,
peaceful, untroubled, like one sleeping. . . . He slipped
to his knees and began to speak to her, telling her how wrong
he had been, how completely wrong, and stupid . . . and
deceitful. . . . He spoke softly, the terrible sincerity of a
despairing contrition in his accents . . . and when she made
no reply, he reached out and took her hand— The lifeless cold
of her unresponsive fingers shocked him back to reality, and
the agony of his loss brought his face down against the chill
flesh of her hand. . . .

The dereliction in his heart was no longer just a numbing
emptiness: it was a dark, bitter, writhing river, spreading

ever wider, thrusting ever deeper, until he seemed drowned in its intolerable flood. . . .

With the instinctive action of the drowning his head came upright, straining to rise above the suffocating flood—but the room was a pitiless well of silence and death and submerging pain. . . . And it was then that he glimpsed, as through a gray mist, the object fastened to the opposite wall—the symbol, its bitter dark wood, eternal in its expressive silence. Slowly the features emerged: the crown-tortured Head, the pain-twisted Body, the arms spread wide—love's gesture, in the midst of loss—utter dereliction with open arms, waiting arms. . . .

Like something wrenched by the roots from his heart, the words then came, a hard, dry whisper of sound in the empty room: "Help me . . . if You can . . . help me . . . I can't, I can't . . . it's too much—take it—" His head came down; and the cold flesh of a dead hand was against his mouth, stopping his cry. . . .

There was no sense of a decision having been made, of a vast frontier having been crossed; there was just a sensation as of a deadly tiredness meeting a vast restfulness, and he let the peace of it enfold him. . . .

The dark insistency of his grief still burned, in the very center of him and all through him; but it burned like a quiet flame, controlled and purposeful. . . . In the warmth of that flame the numbing coldness in his heart seemed to dissolve; and he saw, with absolute clarity, what it was that now remained for him to do. . . . Thought flowed so readily into action that time lapsed. He was not consciously aware that he had gone from the room and returned; there were no longer conflicts and decisions and then action—there were only sensations. So he became aware that the coldness of the dead flesh his hands had held had changed into warmth—and looking down in faint wonderment, he saw the child in his arms. . . .

His gaze went to the bed and the fresh white sheet, molded, like newly fallen snow, about the unmoving form beneath it. Her face alone showed, an infinite remoteness. . . .

Slowly his eyes came away from the lifeless form and turned to the living child in his arms.

The child slept, and the quiet of the child in his arms was like the quiet of the woman on the bed, whom he had so often held in his arms. There was only this slight rise and fall of the child's breast to tell him that the closed eyes, the complete stillness were a counterfeit of death, and not the real thing. . . .

And a strangeness came over him at the realization that he was holding here, in his two arms, the living fruit of a dead love. . . . Dead love? Elaine would not speak, would never smile upon him again. He knew that: and yet there was within him an unbelievably sure sense that their love was not ended. His thought was clear, and somehow, without words, it was directed to and received by her, who could no longer hear with the ears of the body. Love lived on in the child, a child bought with a great price, the child of a love than which there is none greater, for it had loved unto death, and in so doing denied death.

Someone was speaking. As if from a far distance, he heard a voice, a man's voice, and it was an alien sound, for it came from the world of reality.

"The child should be in the nursery. . . . Why did you bring him here?"

Father Chriswell was at his side, the dark, gentle eyes deeply troubled. . . .

"I wanted her to see him," Gray said, "in my arms." And then, with heartbreaking intentness: "You see, I promised her—I promised—"

The priest's arm was suddenly about Gray's shoulder, his voice murmuring understandingly, as he guided him toward the door. . . .

Chapter 26

THE household of Arnet was administered by an elderly, angular spinster. She made no secret of her relief when she admitted Gray to the house. Arnet had been acting strangely: remaining in his room, neglecting his patients, refusing food. . . . If he was sick why did he not let her call a doctor?

Her voluble complaints were no exaggeration. Gray was shocked at Arnet's appearance. He had never seen his friend this way: the robe bunched up about his shoulders, the neck of his shirt unbuttoned, the cheeks unshaven, the face singularly slack looking. . . . He did not know what to say.

Arnet's eyes lifted. They were dull: the narcotic had taken all the icy sureness from the light blue eyes. "I intended to come—I would have come—for Elaine's sake—but. . . ." He held up his hands, and stared at them with fearful eyes.

Gray had not come to reproach Arnet about being absent from the funeral. He was lonely, and Arnet was his friend. In the light of recent experiences he had re-evaluated their friendship. How much Arnet's ideas had influenced him he knew. There was no recrimination in his heart; only a clearer perception of the innate honesty which had motivated his friend . . . and because of that there were things he wished to say.

But when a man is sick you are first a doctor, then a friend. Gray's attempts at medical advice were cut abruptly short. Arnet would handle his own case. . . .

The proud declaration of self-sufficiency Gray found pathetic. Arnet sat before him a prey to fear. His medical knowledge only fed that fear: actualizing as it did the progression of his disease and the crippling pain that lay ahead. . . . And because his body was for Arnet the sum total of reality, life held no longer any other purpose except to deaden the pain of this slow dying. . . .

Surely, Gray thought, the things we scoffed at as religious idealisms—even if they were only that—were they not better than this drab, animal way of dying? They provided a hope, a meaning—this held nothing. And a surge of compassion forced him to speak:

"You were always so intent on right principles, Hil," he observed, "you never ceased telling us the importance of them. 'One error in principle,' you used to say, 'meant thousands of errors in practice.'"

The lackluster eyes focused on him: "After the harm is done, you remember. . . ." There was a dull bitterness in his voice. Only one person could have been a comfort to him in his present trial—Gray had sacrificed her to his ambitions. "You've got what you wanted. . . . Go ahead and enjoy it now. . . ." Gray did not flinch. He had gone much more deeply into his errors than this; and Arnet, not aware of that, tried futilely to twist the knife in the wound: "The research is all yours now—safe and sure. . . . That Sorrento girl can't accuse you—she has no corroboration. Elaine is dead. . . . You paid the price—see if it was worth it. . . ."

Pityingly Gray looked at him. Over Elaine's grave he had heard the chaplain speak a wonderful word. What it had conveyed to him had been very real at the moment; it still was. ". . . Everyone who liveth and believeth in me shall not die for ever. . . ." He had come here, wanting to share with his friend the consolation these words had brought him: the sense that they had been spoken for him and his moment of loss. . . . But now, he asked himself, in the face of Arnet's corrosive bitterness, could he tell him that? How explain that when he had reached out blindly, trustingly, to the love which had thought of him, provided for him (before ever he was born), death's terrors had seemed to fall away? Death was not what he and Arnet had thought it. Death was just a dark door opening into a bright room; it was merely the somber autumn of a glorious unending spring—

But you came to that on your knees, or not at all. . . . He had heard Father Chriswell say that, and it had meant nothing to him then. It did now. All his life Arnet had been self-sufficient—a god, whose intellect and will were the ultimates, and a god bends the knee to no one. . . .

Gray's every attempt to speak was cut short. Futilely, in all subsequent visits, he tried to share with his friend what others had tried futilely, for so long a time, to share with him. Arnet's diamond hard mentality could not yield; it could only be crumbled into dust. And for Gray it was as heartbreaking as being forced to watch a blind man die of thirst because he could not see the well of water in front of him. . . .

With frightening clarity he saw suffering as an inescapable sword of separation, sundering the entire human race: in one camp was the darkness of despair and annihilation; in the other the light of great hope and peace. . . . In the solitude where his own loss had placed him he was surrounded and filled with a mysterious, satisfying quiet that nothing could touch or trouble. The hospital's activity swirled about him: he was part of it, yet apart from it. Despite that, he was aware, time and again, of the murmured word of sympathy, of the kindly glance from a nun or nurse. . . .

Somehow he was no longer just a man endowed with medical skill; he was a *person*. . . . A new relationship had been established between himself and people; it was almost as though people had been drawn, instinctively, to his side at the appearance of the dark foe. And he wondered if this, too, was part of suffering's mysterious purpose, that by means of it mankind should be helped to rediscover their original love and mutual dependence. . . .

Sandra was the sole exception. Whenever he encountered

her, the expression in her eyes, fearful, wary, made him sharply conscious of the agony of suspense in which she must be living. His efforts to determine what he must do about her seemed always to be disrupted by the irrelevant yet persistent memory of a child, a nameless child, with her blond head bowed in grief over a dying father. . . . Having a child of his own would account for his concern about Clayton's fatherless child; but it did not explain why it should always be bound up with the thought of Sandra. The connection when it did appear was so evidently right and simple, that he was moved to immediate action. There seemed an inevitableness now about his actions, even as there was about his thinking. . . . The chaplain was the last one he approached. . . .

With difficulty Father Chriswell attended to Gray's recital. A dust storm had come up from the south, blotting out the brightness of the sky and the clean expanse of the desert behind a pall of swirling yellowish-brown. The thrust of the wind against the pane filled the room with its clamorous importuning, like some invisible force, demanding entrance; . . . but Gray's voice went pitilessly on, reducing, piecemeal, the fiction of his own proud importance to nothingness. . . .

Weather such as this disturbed Father Chriswell: the turmoil of dust and wild wind was so much like life, its confusion and seeming purposelessness. . . . Tenaciously his mind had clung, all these past days, to the mystery of Clayton's inopportune death; trying to understand the wisdom of a design which always escaped him. Repeatedly he had had to remind himself: "My vision is limited. . . . I see only a

tiny segment of the pattern. . . . It is not necessary that I *see*
—only that I believe." A man did not believe if he saw: he
knew. Elaine had not seen the full results of her prayer:
Gray's change of heart had taken place after she was gone.
Yet her faith in the efficacy of prayer had never faltered. . . .

And the miracle of fulfilment was perhaps for that very
reason all the more remarkable. The strong lines of Gray's
countenance held now a quiet dignity, in spite of the humiliating disclosures just made. . . .

"What you intend to do, doctor, is generous," Father
Chriswell said, "but I don't think it is necessary." He pushed
back towards him the large envelop Gray had placed on the
desk. "I think I can convince her without this."

Gray shook his head. He knew Sandra would not listen—
this was the only way.

"You are forgetting something," the priest reminded him,
and then went on, patiently, to point out that since Gray
could now take steps against Sandra with impunity, his open
avowal that he would not do so could have only one significance for her: "You are convinced you made a mistake. In
a moment of anger you made an unjust accusation against
her, which you are now retracting—" Gray's expression
caused him to break off. "You still doubt?"

Gray did not want to gainsay him, but the chaplain had
not fully grasped what drastic measures were required to
effect a change in Sandra. Words had lost all power to influence her: they had betrayed her too deeply. "Due," he
confessed, "to the way I misused them."

Father Chriswell fingered his lower lip. He had no particular pride in his ability to persuade. "But I wish you would allow me to try to convince her." When Gray looked at him inquiringly he admitted that he, personally, wanted Gray to remain here. "The scope of the research requires certain qualities in its personnel if truly great results are to be achieved. I think," he said simply, "that you now have, at the very least, an understanding of what those qualities are."

Faint color reddened Gray's face: "I can't remain, Father," he said in a low voice. "No matter what Sandra does or doesn't do, I must sever all connections with research work. . . . It's something I've got to do, Father, believe me. . . ."

Intently the priest's gaze studied him. "I do believe you," he said, and picking up the envelop he placed it in a drawer.

Haltingly, Gray tried to explain. He had come upon a great truth, and a grubby-faced boy with a burned hand seemed to have had some part in it. "Love is not greatness," he said slowly, "no matter how deep it may be—unless it has extension. . . ." From that starting-point a number of practical consequences had been derived. Patiently, Father Chriswell pieced together what Gray was trying to say: no man was a self-contained little world; he was an individual, yes, but an individual member of a family. Whatever joy or sorrow happened to an individual affected the whole family. The harm he had done to Sandra could not be expiated merely by repairing the damage done to her. The harm was wider than that, the expiation had to be wider—

The priest interrupted him: "You can't have a family," he cautioned, "without a Father." When Gray nodded his understanding of that and his acceptance, the priest became suddenly silent. By what simple yet potent means had Gray been led to that great basic truth? A boy with an injured hand, the example and prayers of his wife—

"If you are wondering, Father, about a man like me," Gray said; "that I, of all people, should talk this way—"

"Nothing like that crossed my mind," Father Chriswell assured him. "Nothing—truly." And when Gray's expression did not change. "I was thinking of Clayton," he blurted out. Gray's countenance showed open puzzlement. "Everything seems to stem from his having been your patient—" He broke off, his eyes showing an embarrassment unusual to him. And Gray, remembering Father Chriswell's concern and dejection the night of Clayton's death, wondered whether that tragic event which had so powerfully altered his own career had also, in some unknown way, affected the chaplain. . . . Father Chriswell looked up at him: "It seems, doctor," he observed, "that 'God still writes straight, with crooked lines.'" He made no attempt to connect the proverb with his sudden and unusual embarrassment, but gestured towards the drawer containing the envelop. "I will take care of that matter for you, doctor, in the way you wish."

Father Chriswell did not have to summon Sandra. She came, early the following day, to see him of her own accord. He was not surprised: it seemed but another segment of a complicated pattern unfolding surely and inevitably. Her hair was neatly combed, her face youthfully fresh, her uniform immaculate—but her eyes were harried and unhappy. . . .

Elaine's death had been a shocking blow, ending her period
of dark gloating triumph. She no longer held Gray in the
hollow of her hand. The tables were turned, and he was
subjecting her to the same cruel waiting which she had inflicted upon him. . . . "Why," she asked herself frantically,
"did I delay? I had the chance, and, like a fool, I threw it
away." Was it because she thought Elaine would not die?
Yes; that was it. She had not really believed Elaine would
die; and it was Gray's hard, forceful assurance (that night
on the roof) that Elaine would not die, that he would see
to it that she did not die, which had influenced her. "I
waited," she told herself, "because I wanted him to make
good his proud boast. Then I would have taken action."
Elaine's witnessing of his loss of prestige and position would
have made it so much more intolerable for Gray. Through
Elaine he could be hurt most—or had it been in the back of
her mind to make Elaine, too, suffer? She pushed that
thought aside: the only thing of importance now was that
she *had* waited too long; she was in Gray's power. . . .

The tip of her tongue moistened her lips repeatedly as she
spoke. And she spoke quietly, but her denunciation of Gray
was like the slash of a claw, short, deadly, and merciless.
Father Chriswell's face remained expressionless: Gray's
calm recital had been so much more pitiless than this savage attack. . . .

"Your professional integrity," he observed quietly, "means
everything to you." His slight pause gave her the chance to
deny the statement if she wished. "Why then do you not

leave? Obtain a position in some other hospital before any accusation is—"

"Because I have to know," she interrupted, her voice desperate, "whether I am guilty of Elaine's death. . . ." Her fingers interlocked tightly. "Did I really want to save the child's life and keep Gray from being a murderer—or was I just saying that . . . hiding in back of it . . . so I could see Elaine die?" She looked up at him her face all twisted with emotion: "You know the whole story now—tell me—I must know, I've got to know. . . ."

Her passionate cry did not seem to touch him: "Why," he asked, "is it so imperative that you *know*?"

She turned her eyes full upon him, and they were sick with frustration and desire. "Don't you understand? . . . I can't live without knowing what I really am—" She broke off, as the full weight of her destroying doubt overwhelmed her. Was she some inhuman monster or a martyr? Distractedly the palms of her hands pressed against her temples. "His accusation is driving me insane. . . . I can't face him unless I know. . . . Don't you—can't you see?"

He nodded.

"You are very much in love with him."

"Love him? . . . I hate him!"

He shook his head slowly in denial: "You could have ruined him—you did not: because that would have sent him away, and you could not bear the thought of being separated from him." Her hands dropped to the arms of her chair, and her eyes burned hot with indignant denial. "This infatuation of

231

yours is blinding you to the truth," he went on calmly. "You
are not concerned about whether you did or did not kill
Elaine—you are tortured about what he thinks of you." He
held up a hand, forestalling the violent repudiation trembling on her lips. Gray's accusation had put her on the same
level as he; and that made it impossible for her to approach
him. ". . . Because you know that he can only love someone who is above him . . . he is made that way . . . greatness he loves . . . and he loved Elaine because he found a
quality of greatness in her—"

"Do you want to hurt the one you love?" she retorted.

"No; of course not." He had used the word loosely when
speaking of her attraction for Gray. More exactly he had
called it infatuation; and infatuation resorted to measures
which genuine love would never even think of. . . . Angrily,
she brushed all that aside. She had not come here to have
her feelings toward Dr. Powers analyzed. She wanted an
opinion, his opinion, on whether she had done right or
wrong. . . .

Patiently the priest shook his head:

"What you really want is his opinion—not mine. . . ."

Her glance darted up to him: "His opinion means nothing
to me. . . . He could swear on a stack of Bibles, and I would
not believe him."

Gentle skepticism showed in Father Chriswell's eyes. "You
believed him when he accused you of wanting to see Elaine
die—why don't you believe him when he revokes that judgment?" He saw the questioning in her eyes. "He has already

done that," he assured her, "or tried to, by resigning from the research."

"And by giving me back the evidence against me," she added quickly. "Tricks, both of them—to buy my silence."

"Your silence means nothing now," he pointed out. "You may speak or not—your words will have no corroboration. He can harm you; you can't harm him." Her silence indicated her awareness of that fact. "He resigned his position . . . yesterday."

There was no doubting the shocked disbelief that stiffened her features. "He didn't," she denied, with dry lips.

"I was present when Dr. Bromwell accepted it."

There was a moment of silence; then the cynical glint that came into her eyes told the priest she had adjusted herself to this unexpected development: Gray had received an offer from some other institution, a more profitable and attractive one. She looked up at the chaplain wanting corroboration.

Father Chriswell shook his head:

"Gray is finished with research," he said, "completely finished." With great deliberateness, he unfolded a legal-looking document and began to explain its contents: the financial returns from the use of his father's formula were to be used for the upbringing of Clayton's child; the administration of that trust was to be offered to Sandra and to facilitate that, a position was offered her caring for the patients the research would handle. . . . The child for the time being was to be placed in a boarding-school. . . .

She had made no attempt to interrupt him, but the odd expression in her countenance caused the priest vague misgivings. "He feels this responsibility deeply," he explained. "His offering it to you is an evidence of his complete trust in you." She still had made no sign of acceptance. "There is, too, security for yourself and for the child—"

She reached forward and took the document. "When does he plan to leave?" she asked. Father Chriswell told her: tomorrow morning, early.

"Time enough for me to thank him?" she suggested.

Father Chriswell's deeply-shadowed eyes fixed intently upon her. "It is not thanks that he expects or looks for—of that I am certain."

She stood up quickly: "I shall see him before he leaves," she said, and the lack of inflection in her voice seemed to give an import which the words themselves did not contain.

For a long time, the priest sat staring at the empty seat opposite, realizing how truly Gray had assessed this girl. Plainly a favor at Gray's hands was for her unthinkable. Recalling the details Gray had given him about her, he could see how, by meeting Gray, her disillusionment with the false loves of her early life had been replaced by an eager hope. The things Gray then told her (not believing them himself at the time) had made real to her in his own person, a love she had always dreamed of with its warmth of affection, its idealisms and security. Being a person avid for love, she had surrendered wholeheartedly to his attraction; and once committed it was impossible for her to alter or interrupt her course. The deceit Gray had practised upon her she hated,

234

savagely and wholeheartedly; yet she remained inextricably, hopelessly bound to him. . . . Sadly Father Chriswell shook his head: he had read of this type of passion, understanding little of it; but Sandra's words and behavior made many things clear and real. A strange reversal had taken place in her love for Gray: if she could not have him, then she would hurt him. As passionately as she had loved, now she virulently hated. Of that he was certain; and because he had no idea what direction this misguided passion of Sandra's now would take, he was a prey to vague fears for Gray's safety.

Chapter 27

ONCE, at the moment of vital decision, Sandra had committed a drastic blunder: she had hidden in the dark of a chapel and allowed shadowy emotions to be the arbiters of her fate. She would never repeat that mistake. Among the living was the place to decide about life, not among the dead.

Their table was in a remote corner, and the talk of the other diners, and the background of soft music from a good orchestra made for privacy without isolation. It was exactly what she had desired.

She smiled across the rim of her glass. If things had been

different she could have thoroughly enjoyed this moment. But Dr. Reynolds was no substitute for Gray. His close-cropped hair and well-scrubbed face made him seem the eternal sophomore. He never had interested her, but there was something she needed from him. "You think that he really intends to leave?" she asked.

Carefully, Ralph put down his glass. If he had wondered why Sandra had maneuvered him into this evening conversation, her line of conversation had quickly cleared up matters. His shrewd young eyes had seen much farther than Sandra imagined, and being a naturally kindly person he hated what he would have to say to her. "I don't think he is leaving, Sandra," he said, ". . . I know." He hesitated a split second: "I helped him pack."

If she was shocked she gave no evidence of it: "That need not be final," she suggested. "Dr. Powers could change his mind at the last moment."

It was pitiful the way she still grasped at straws. He shook his head: "He has already handed in his resignation. . . . Bromwell accepted it—" The look that tightened her features stopped him: "Didn't you know? It is all over the hospital now."

Her gaze fixed itself unseeingly on the table: "I had heard something to that effect," she admitted. "But I still cannot believe it. . . . Why should he do this?" She hesitated, as though the utter lack of reasons made further speech impossible. "He can't do it!" she suddenly exclaimed with low vehemence: "The research is part of him; he can't give it up. It's . . . it's food and drink to him, it's his life." Her eyes lifted to his. "You know that: you were very close to him."

Ralph nodded. His relationship to Gray had always been a matter of pride to him, and her appeal to it as a matter of course subtly flattered him. But it did not make his task any easier. He had to disillusion her. There was no vestige of hope remaining for her. "Maybe what happened in the hospital—memories, tragic memories—would be too much for him—" He interrupted himself and shrugged: "You have no idea how much he loved his wife." She winced visibly at that, and he hastily tried to soften the blow. Gray had a sort of one-track mind, most great men did (maybe that was what made a man great), and it was a trait that could bring tragedy. Gray would never return to this hospital, because here he could never forget Elaine. He probably would never forget her, no matter where he went: and if ever he re-married, his new wife would be competing all her life with the memory of the dead Elaine. . . . "All of that does not contradict what you said," he explained. "The research *was* everything to him—but not," he hastened to add, "in any selfish or personal way." Her eyes were fixed intently on his now; and he thought they held a definite questioning. "What the research would accomplish for the sick," he explained, "meant more to him than personal success—that's why he left his notes and his whole theory of a cure—"

"Who told you that?"

The question startled him. "Why, Bromwell did." Dr. Reynolds had been trying to convince him that he could prevail on Gray to stay if he told Gray that the research, left without a program, would be a failure. "That's taken care of," Bromwell had blurted out. "He left his notes."

"I find that hard to believe."

Her desperate refusal to face the truth was pitiable: but he had told her nothing but the truth. He had checked Dr. Bromwell's disclosure with Gray. "Gray admitted it," he said, "reluctantly. . . ."

"But he did admit it . . . and plainly?"

He nodded assent; and as he looked at her an odd expression seemed to dawn in her eyes. But at the moment the lights were dimming while a spot picked up a singer standing near the microphone. He could not be quite sure; the expression on Sandra's face almost seemed like satisfaction—which patently was absurd.

He leaned forward, but her eyes had closed, and her head was held slightly back in an attitude of rapt listening. The contralto at the microphone was singing throatily: "Because God made thee mine . . . I'll cherish thee . . . through light and darkness, through all time to be. . . ."

A faraway look, a dreaminess had come over Sandra's features; the white of her face looked beautiful in the dim light. He reached forward and covered her hand, hesitantly, with his own. The ghost of a tender smile touched her lips; and she did not withdraw her hand. At the moment she felt profoundly grateful to this unimportant little man who had unknowingly solved her all-important problem.

It was lucidly clear what Gray meant to do and why.

Behind her closed lids she saw again the chaplain's face and its bewilderment because she had been so unfeeling about Gray's generosity. . . . It was of a piece with the gullibility of the youth holding her hand. Never having been in love what could they know of passion's hidden depths? Their simple faith took Gray's actions at face value. . . . The poor deluded fools did not know the first thing about Gray. She alone knew him: all the deeps, the twistings and turnings of his devious desires. . . . Her love made his every move as plain to her as an open book: and the sureness of her knowledge delivered him into her hands. . . .

Deep down in his heart was the reality which Gray could not escape: he was a shoddy trickster, a little man whom forces larger than he had laughed at, defeated, and made a fool of. *She, too, knew that.* And while he might succeed, if left to himself, in closing his eyes to the inner reality, he could never succeed in blotting it out permanently as long as her presence was there to remind him. So he was fleeing the sight of her. He would make a great gesture of nobility, and then disappear. . . . But that, she told herself with grim satisfaction, is something I will stop. If he thinks he is going to make his exit in a blaze of glory how little he knows me! It was all beautifully clear to her at that moment: all his life Gray had looked up to Elaine. It was a fixation now; a necessity for him. And Sandra would arrange very simply for its continuance—but it would be to her he would look, during the remainder of his life. . . .

The pressure of Ralph's hand caused her eyes to open. The singer was taking a bow, and Sandra withdrew her hand to join in the applause. As the lights came up she gave her escort a prettily contrite look: "The music . . . I'm sorry," and she began to talk very volubly. . . .

They rode home with the top of the convertible down. The evening was warm and lovely with stars. Sandra's head lay back against the cushions, her mood of talkativeness ended. It seemed to her she had but to reach up a hand and she could pluck the stars like flowers.

Ralph asked if she had enjoyed the evening. She sat up, turned to him with a relaxed, easy smile, thanking him for an enjoyable time.

The road was free of cars. At the end of it, far away, stood the hospital, the illuminated cross atop of it hanging like a portent in the vast emptiness of the night sky. She could not take her eyes from it: "It looks so serene," she murmured, "almost beautiful—from the outside."

The final phrase caused Reynolds to turn his head sharply. Her faintly cynical glance told him he had not misunderstood—and suddenly he did not like her very much. Cynical people annoyed him—no matter how good-looking they might be. Sure, there were unpleasant duties to be performed inside that pleasant-looking building: the bright-windowed rooms held diseased and broken bodies. You found that out very quickly; and you either stayed with it or you quit. "It's our job," he stated sturdily; and to him that meant going about among those aching, sweating, decaying bodies, and doing what you were supposed to do. If you wanted beautiful landscapes—

241

She made no attempt to reply. He was just a stuffy little sophomore, as she had always known. To try to explain to him why she despised this stodgy old building would have been an utter waste of time. Its supposedly high-minded ideals were a myth. She had learned; whereas he never would. This gleaming edifice was nothing but a smelly factory for patching up broken, misused, worn-out flesh. That was all it was. The rest of its claims were all a fraud. And she was going to use its fraud to escape, to get for herself all the things that were real and worthwhile in life. . . .

"Always bad to talk shop," Ralph was saying apologetically as he swung the car off the highway in the direction of her apartment. "I'm a bit of a fanatic on some things. . . ."

She let him prattle on. . . . He was unimportant. . . . He had served his purpose. . . .

Chapter 28

THE crisp of early morning was in the air as Sandra walked toward the main entrance of the hospital. For the first time in many weeks she had slept well; and now it needed but a good breakfast in the hospital cafeteria to ready her for what she was about to do.

A shoulder-bag swung jauntily at her side as she stepped briskly up the main approach, the tapping of her high heels sounding surprisingly sharp in the thin still air. The parking lot had only a few empty cars in it. A man was bent busily over the trunk of one of them, and as she came abreast he straightened up. She halted. At the same moment he turned and recognized her. There was no doubting the look of joyful surprise that swept over his face as he spoke her name.

A little start of fear shot through her: she had almost

missed him! She could see the trunk; it was neatly filled with luggage.

"It was good of you, Sandra," he said . . . and then, hesitantly: "Or am I being presumptuous? . . . Since you're not in uniform—"

She admitted that she had come early on purpose to see him, expecting to catch him at his office. . . . There was something she had to say to him.

"There isn't anything you have to say, Sandra," he replied simply. "I'm more happy than I can tell you, just because you came to say good-by."

Faint puzzlement put a thin line between her brows. He spoke so sincerely. . . . She had not counted on him expecting her to appear! But of course, it fitted. Her grateful farewell was to be part of his great renunciation act; the grand climax in fact—she to be singing his praises as he departed. If he only knew!

"I should have seen you yesterday," she said apologetically, "I wanted to—but my feelings got the better of me—"

The light that came into his eyes betrayed him. He would have dawdled around here for hours until she came! He would never change: a big front, but behind it a little man and his squirming deceits. . . . But such as he was, he was hers, and she was going to have him for her own.

"I . . . I can't say fully what this has meant to me," she began. "Your generosity towards me and Clayton's daughter is too great for words. . . ." She was fumbling inside of her shoulder bag, and so she did not see the sudden sharp change that swept across his countenance. Her fingers had found the envelope. "This is what you gave to Father Chriswell for me." She was all suppliant pleading as she held it towards him: "You must take it back, Gray . . . I can't accept it. . . . Grateful as I am, it would haunt me all my life to think that I have kept you from the great task which the world waits for you to perform—" His blank expression caused her to break off. "Oh, don't you understand? I am not important—but *you* are, to medical science, to the sick, to the world."

For a long moment he studied her and a sadness seemed to come over him. "I meant for you to have this, Sandra," he said quietly, "and to keep it. I did mean that."

"Of course . . . I understand that—but there is no need for me to have it. . . . I am content that you should have *wanted* to give me what means so much to you. . . ."

He could not pierce through to her purpose, but he knew, instinctively and surely, that his final effort had failed. Heavily he turned, and the lid of the trunk made a lifeless thud as he closed it.

"You don't understand, Sandra," he said with a horrible sort of beaten patience: "*Nothing* will change my decision. . . . I am going away."

Before she could make a reply he was walking away from her toward the front of the car. Faintly alarmed she started after him, but came to a full sudden stop. She could see the front seat of the car, and the tiny red face looking out from its cocoon of blankets. . . . The child! All bundled up for traveling! . . . Something snapped inside of her. She had hold of his hand and was trying to thrust the document into it: "Take it . . . please, Gray . . . I mean it now, really mean it. . . . I'll never open my lips—I don't care what you think of me—only stay. . . ."

"I'm . . . I'm sorry, Sandra. . . ." His voice was strangely low and rough with emotion. ". . . More sorry than I can ever tell you. . . ."

It broke on her with sickening suddenness: she was about to lose him! "Please, Gray . . . don't go . . . I beg of you— you can't go—" A warm clot in her throat seemed suddenly choking her. He stood there quietly, saying nothing, his eyes filled with wordless compassion and sorrow because her need for him was something he could not do anything for. . . . "Where?" she whispered. "Where are you going? . . ."

"If I told you, I'm afraid you wouldn't believe—much less understand—"

"Tell me," she demanded fiercely. "I must know . . . I've got a right to know. . . . Where are you going?"

"Some little place, any little place . . . where there are little people, needy people—" He said it simply, but the strange light that kindled in his eyes told her the compulsion of some great purpose was burning in him like a flame. . . . Her one little need, was swallowed up in the vision of those many other needy ones. . . .

She drew slightly away from him, her eyes filled with startled wonderment. The man she had dreamed of, the man she wanted, really existed! He was here, now, before her eyes —and suddenly all the things he had told her were real again. A wild exultant happiness thrilled through her, making her want to cry and to laugh and to sing.

He had reached forth a hand to open the door, but she thrust herself in front of him: "Oh, no, no, Gray . . . not now. . . . You cannot leave me—" Faintly bewildered the gray-blue eyes looked deeply into hers. Surely she, who had recently mounted the hill of heroism, would know the mystery and rewards of that rough road. . . . It puzzled him that she should be attempting to dissuade him from the greatness she herself had attained—

With utter sincerity he had placed her on a pedestal, far above himself—and her only sensation was a suffocating frenzy of futility. She could not plead her own love: it was selfish; she was false to his belief in her if she did. . . . Despairingly, her hand groped upwards on his arm: "But the child, Gray . . . your own child—you can't—"

He shook his head slowly. The child was included in whatever he had in mind; he wanted the child to have what his own father had given to him. And when she clung to him, begging him to explain, he stressed each word of his reply: "You learn best the things you see lived."

In the savagery of her defeat she wanted to throw herself upon him and scream aloud her need of him, her right to him; but he moved away from her, and her nerveless fingers made no attempt to restrain him. . . . She scarce heard his farewells, the tranquil assurances. . . . Through a blur of tears she saw the car draw away, and disappear in the distance. . . . In her hand she still held the envelope with its guarantee of security, which once had meant everything to her—now she wanted to shred it into pieces. . . .

Slowly she turned. The hospital bulked large before her,

and looking at it she hated it. For it was this heap of insensate stone and steel which had changed Gray, making him into the kind of man he had once posed as being: the kind of man she wanted him to be—truly great—and by doing that, it had placed him beyond her reach. . . . And the irony of it bit deep into her soul: for she was condemned to stay here, to live here, an integral part of this hospital's fulfilling love, while her own heart was filled with the emptiness of hate. . . .

The sun had mounted the rim of the distant mountains, and its first rays seemed to strike downward across the desert and focus on the building. All the blinding brilliancy of its light struck the walls, and turned them into something unbelievably beautiful to behold. The windows were molten squares of shattering light set in gleaming snow. The entire edifice was become a city of God, standing in intolerable beauty between the dust brown drabness of the earth and the thin blue greatness of the skies. It was no longer a house of sordid suffering but a mount of transfiguration.

And as she stood there looking upon it, the intolerable brilliance of the light gradually faded, and it was again a thing of solemn stone and whiteness, set on the outskirts of the town where the streets of the city ended and the desert began.

She began walking toward it, while far off and faint sounded the thin wail of the ambulance's siren . . . and the hospital stood there stolidly strong, in its silence and sureness, waiting.